WRITING 40

Edward Dorn

VIEWS

Edited by Donald Allen

Four Seasons Foundation
San Francisco • 1980

The Poet, the People, the Spirit was first published by Talonbooks,
Vancouver, in 1976.

LIBRARY OF CONGRESS
CATALOGING IN PUBLICATION DATA

Dorn, Edward.
    Views.

    (The Writing series ; 40)
    I. Title.
PS3507.073277V5   810.9'0054   79-25498
ISBN 0-87704-50-8
ISBN 0-87704-51-6 pbk.

Typesetting: David Mattingly
Design: George Mattingly & Donald Allen

The publication of this book was partially supported by a grant from
the National Endowment for the Arts, Washington, D.C., a federal agency.

No man sets himself about any
thing, but upon some *view* or other,
which serves him for reason.

                          –Locke

Contents

Ed Dorn's Views

What follows is a transcript of a discussion between myself
and Ed Dorn in Boulder, February 1980. Ed's "views," as so
succinctly stated (or, in his term, alarmingly suggested) in the
prose of this book, are what they are, and this interview does
not so much attempt to elucidate them as to coax from their
author some observations on the thinking behind them—and
on how that's changed over the years. My own part in this is
peripheral. The early Dorn essays in *Migrant, Measure, Yūgen,
Kulchur,* and other more-or-less fugitive magazines, appearing
in the 1960s, seemed to me then the best semi-occasional
writing of their day. I subsequently had the luck of having Ed
write some of the later pieces in this book for magazines I was
editing—*The Wivenhoe Park Review* and *Boulder Monthly.*
Would that I were still editing magazines, and he would be
writing again for me now. Anyway, I'm honored to regard the
man as a friend, find his views of great interest at all times,
and hope that the interview that follows helps you enjoy
them.

TOM CLARK

Q. "What I See In *The Maximus Poems*" has always seemed to me a very eloquent prose statement of your principles and conditions as a writer, whereas the later and more occasional pieces here tend to take those same principles and conditions you've stated, and employ them more locally.

A. The "Maximus" essay represents a transition from an earlier more statemental kind of prose to a kind of alarming suggestion that came later.

Q. So you think of the pieces in this book as essays?

A. I do think of them as essays. They seem essays in the sense that that would be the best thing they would get to be.

Q. Have you consciously thought about the art of the essay, as a special form, while you were writing these pieces?

A. I haven't thought about the question of the essay, directly, so much as made an attempt to imitate, or emulate perhaps, or *copy* even, the highest voices I ever heard when I was reading. Sometimes that didn't get to be style, because when you're doing that, a lot of voices enter.

Q. In the form of the nonfiction prose "view" is there any writer you can think of who's been strong in your mind as a master of that form?

A. Absolutely. The styles I most admire—actually, Dr. Johnson's not one of them. Because he's a little too inhibited by the *necessity* of style, in a way. Although I enjoy reading him, I wouldn't actually copy him. But people like Hazlitt and Oliver Goldsmith seem to be more reasonable as models.

Q. Johnson's style has a lot of imposed requirements, for balance. Somewhat unconsciously, but also intentionally, he strives for balance in his sentences. If you look at that style in terms of geometrical shape, there'd be equal placements on both sides of a center. And in terms of logic, a counter-argument's given for every argument made. This classical stylistic principle exists in both his syntax and his ideas. Whereas, in your essay on Douglas Woolf you describe Woolf's style, in geometrical space imagery, as a linear movement with a hook on the end. Isn't Woolf's—or your—open-ended linear proposition very much opposed to this conscious desire for balance of Johnson's?

A. With Woolf, I always admired his sentence, in the way he provoked more than he was ever going to include. The problem with Johnson for me is that he so initiates high style for so many years ahead of him. It's like Edison looking at the first light bulb, which was a beautiful thing. It was hand-blown, the filament was hand-made. And everybody stood around and it was plugged in and it lit up—and that was a great moment. That's like Johnson. Not that anybody could do that particular thing again, because after that there'd be many light bulbs. That's why I think that he's got no useful *praxis* behind him. What he does is just shine forth as the possibility of expression.

Q. Style aside, there's Johnson's confidence that his function as a writer is to take in the accumulation of human reality, as yielded by his own experience, and to assume that this qualifies him to make these free-roving comments about the human condition in general. This seems to be close to what the basic form of the speculative essay is all about, and it also seems to be what's going on in your pieces in this book.

A. Oh, I think that what Johnson actually did, everybody should always try to do. All I was saying was that there is a peculiarity in the sense that he invented criticism, in the *Lives of the Poets,* by putting it so high in the first place that there was never any going back. That's like an ideal, rather than something to be emulated. Everybody after that speaks in a different way. But there are on the other hand certain *common* styles, which are just fine. I think of Hazlitt's, which is just like easy intelligence flowing along a line. Which might be *anybody's* possibility. I mean, in other words, I'm talking about two different *values*.

Q. When you say that Woolf's technique is to provoke more than he includes isn't that really a description of irony?

A. I think so. I think he's the ultimate ironic writer. Which is a thing I've always valued, against the current of my time.

Q. In a sentence like the one in this book that says the bill of fare for wild dogs in Wyoming "will increase on a graph rising with extraction," doesn't that pairing of predatory advantage and mineral extraction "provoke more than it includes" in a way that's radical to your whole intention as a writer?

A. It hopes to. It hopes to provoke a lot.

Q. What do you think that rising graph of extraction means for the West, in terms of your statement here that the West has never been industrialized?

A. The image of that is that since all it's got is what it has, and that's—at the same time the West's very *thin,* when you take it at the optical surface level, like looking at the plains, the prairie, the mountains—when you take it in the sense of what you would look at, that's very, very thin. Its richness is its depth. So it's like the ultimate technical country in a way. You can't get *to* it. There's nothing on top. So high-tech means you've got to go beneath. And so that's its present life. And that's its future, in the sense that its future is short. But it's obviously going to be brilliant. Which it always was. That's the thing that interests us in the West. It's always got a short future, and that future is always brilliant. But it's never going to last. I mean you can only put—every kid knows, when he's sucking up a chocolate soda, that you get to the bottom of it. And then you hear all those last *shlupps*. . .

Q. Of exhaustion?

A. That's right, exhaustion. Whereas, on the other hand, even though the Midwest, for instance, is like the East, being largely abandoned—it's going to the Southern Rim, or it's going to the Coast, or wherever it's going, it's always fleeing in this geometric way—on the other hand, it's the place that's always the richest. Because it's got surface, depth of surface. That's the whole meaning of the prairie. It took millions of years of Nebraska, Kansas, Illinois glaciers coming down and making this the broadest river plain that ever was. Which is called the prairie, and it was six feet of loam.

Q. You've said the Easterner always has his eye out to use the West. In *Hello, La Jolla* you call it "the soil of transport"— taking the East's runoff.

A. Exactly. The problem here is that metals, or let's say minerals, have always been speculation, from the beginning. Dirt, rich dirt, has always been stable—it's always been home. And those are the two different propositions. And the West is being used in that sense right now. It's speculation. But it was in the beginning. You know, most of those early fortunes were. The Wurlitzer fortune was gold before it was jukeboxes.

Q. In your essays you differentiate the westward pioneer group movement associated with property retention, which you see as being the principal vector in our "conquest" of the West, from the non-property-owning, alienated, excluded, nowhere-to-go stranger character who is the lonesome cowboy. This latter figure comes up here and there all through your work. A character like Buck in your story "C B & Q" seems to be a last faded representative of this lonesome cowboy tradition. He doesn't have a horse anymore to get on, but he could always get in his car and drive somewhere because the back seat comes out. This is in the 50s. Where, now, in this gradually depleted surface of the West, is this cowboy figure going to go? Is it still real?

A. That figure is always real. That figure will never disappear. That's the *only* figure that represents the rectitude of the human condition. And when it goes, it won't even be noticed to go—because there won't be anybody to notice it go.

Q. You've moved around the West yourself for much of the last 30 years or so, in a condition that I guess could be described as that of an itinerant worker.

A. I've fought for migration. You see I think the West is where the subservient class in America has traditionally always been replaced by somebody else, like the Haitians are replacing the Puerto Ricans in New York right now. Because of certain territorial-historical facts, this has been territory that has been held by various groups. Somehow the Apaches penetrated the whole thing several thousand years ago and got down to the border. And they're like a droplet off of the Athabaskan situation. Then the Spanish-Mexican came up and couldn't hold it, before American Manifest Destiny. This is just like literally orthodox history. And now the last of the type has been in some sense merged in a grand migratory effect. This whole thing is being ruled by Texas. This is the Texas nation. I mean, everybody should stop kidding themselves, and forget California, and realize that there's these two things happening here. It's like what's left of what *used* to be happening—and now it's Texas. And it goes all the way to Alaska. Every time it happens, it's called the final shot. Dallas. It's *never* the final shot. I mean, there is no *way* to get rid of the cowboy. It's literally Star Wars.

Q. The burden on the back of the traveling cowboy is great. You say an odyssey story can never refer away from the tangent of a single individual. And that the cowboy lives this lonely odyssey. Because in the terrain he's in, homes can't be established. So it'd be absurd for him to attempt to do so. It'd be a waste of time. He knows this.

A. Right. It just comes down to really a single kind of Greek fact, which is that the masses never imagine the universe. It's the one thing they don't do. And it's the one thing they're incapable of. And that's why there even *is* an individual.

Q. So as one who's moved from station to station around the West without more than a few years of respite from what's been in effect migratory work, although maybe a more intellectual migratory work, do you see the distance that's built into that life, the feeling of being doomed to spend it in remote places, always leaving friends behind, as being pretty close to the cowboy story?

A. It is. I grew up in the time when all boys played cowboys and Indians. Somebody who's not at all a cowboy, Van Wyck Brooks, told me a long time ago that I would never be a successful writer—in the sense that a plumber is a successful plumber. So I just kept going. You know, it's like—what is it? I *believe* in the insensitivity of America. I think it's one of the great experiences of the world. It never occurred to me that I couldn't sell my mind to keep myself going in order to write.

Q. How much money do you suspect all these pieces in this book got you, in terms of earnings, at the time you wrote them?

A. Well, certainly I was paid for none of the early pieces. None of the middle pieces. Actually only for the last three or four.

Q. You made a total of two hundred dollars, maybe?

A. That'd be an exaggeration.

Q. A hundred and fifty?

A. Yeah, a hundred and fifty.

Q. Were most of the pieces in this book provoked by an assignment or request of one kind or another?

A. They started out as the purest form of self-assignment. I never had the feeling that I had to wait around for somebody to assign me something to write about. But on the other hand, if you do that, if you prove that *that's* all true, then it'd probably be pretty good for you to be assigned something. Because in fact assignment becomes more and more important as you mature as a writer. There's no doubt about it. In fact, the more you mature as a writer, the *less* you want to invent your own products and the more you want to be given them, to show what you can do.

Q. In a hypothetical case, if it had turned out that assignments were available to you, for example if somebody had asked you to write a book on the West, or on the eighteenth century, or essays also—I take it you'd like to have had more access to that kind of work than you've had?

A. I think it would have been very good for me.

Q. What do you think you'd have had to do to get those kinds of opportunities? I mean to be paid in advance, to have propositions made that wouldn't require you to go through stringent personal circumstances in order to write?

A. An airline ticket to São Paulo?

Q. Yeah, that kind of thing.

A. Exactly! You know, I can't *imagine* what I'd have had to do to get that.

Q. The position you'd have had to put yourself in to get that, wouldn't it have been pretty hard to relate to this other migratory condition?

A. I don't know, it might have been fantastic for me to have put myself in such a position. I was told, kind of—you know, in the early 50s when I was being told—that actually that didn't even come into it. That all this was very serious work. It didn't involve such, you know, delightful exceptions as traveling. So I didn't even grow up in fact assuming that that was even possible.

Q. It does seem that in the last 5 or 6 pieces in the book you are able to use your intelligence in this free-roving eighteenth-century way, to not discriminate the perimeters of your interest—assuming the eighteenth-century principle that all civilized men have interests in common, and that as a writer you should be able to take on anything. So these last few pieces aren't composed so much out of a burning interest on your part as out of the occasional circumstance of an assignment?

A. That's true. But on the other hand I don't think I exercised my intelligence so much. I exercised my imagination, a little bit. You know, where I grew up, I don't think one was that encouraged to use the imagination. It was really not profitable, actually.

Q. You've stated your sense of interest in and affinity with the eighteenth-century mind. What do you think of the Romantics? They're in much higher favor among poets these days.

A. The Romantics are finally like early Whole Earth Catalog. They're really extremely careful. They finally talk about *nothing,* when it comes right down to it. Wordsworth, Shelley . . . Byron, on the other hand, was extremely different. He had style. And in my mind, style excuses everything. A guy like Keats, for instance, obviously lacked style. But he had art. And in my mind, *art* excuses everything. And I don't really—for instance, of those people, the *mind* I'm interested in would be Coleridge. Because he's got the mind. But he's got no style. And he's got no art. And that's the way I think about those values. And I feel extremely anticritical in that sense. I think it actually *is* the way it looks. And I don't think there's any other thing about it.

Q. Going back to the survival of this lonesome cowboy figure, hasn't the position of the itinerant individual in the West changed since, say, the days of your Berkeley speech? It's no longer possible to even exist at survival level in the West—or anywhere in the U.S.—without making the kind of money that used to qualify one as wealthy. If, as you say here, someone in this country is an American only insofar as he has money, then nowadays no one has a choice whether or not to be an American. Everyone has to be, to live.

A. It's turned into an increasing no-choice.

Q. It's getting harder and harder for a character like Buck, who wants to just throw everything in the car and move, to actually live.

A. But we can see the peripheries of this economic situation. Nothing changes the West. The West changes everything. It makes everything that comes to the West, the West. To a certain extent California does, as well.

Q. There's an awful lot of room in places like Arizona for populations still to come. A lot of space. So the West should be able to last a lot longer than certain stress points in our structure.

A. It can last forever. It really sheds itself of the people who can't hang on to it, very rapidly. You know, a lot more people arrive here than stay. An awful lot stay. Even more are leaving. That was always true.

Q. But the West does remain an identifiable place and an identifiable experience, regardless of changes that may be happening because of energy, economics and so on.

A. Europe, and northern Europe in particular, has always clarified its propositions as to tensions, in terms of greater space. That was the first reason for people even to—I mean, that's the meaning of the westward expansion, really. And so, after the great westward expansion, which was actually the Elizabethan expansion, then you got the trans-Appalachian expansion, and then you got the last expansion. But we're still having a jillion mini-expansions. I mean, it keeps expanding inside itself, because that's its nature. Otherwise, why would somebody in a 4 by 4 travel three hours to his job and when he goes home at night maybe can't make the last mile and a half, most of the time.

Q. The Greeks, here, the Odyssey, Hector and the Greek experience—in these essays you relate this Greek experience to the Western one. Where did that tie-in come from?

A. Certainly one of the books that had a great influence on me was Nietzsche's work on the Pre-Socratics, which is excellent—one of the great books that I know of. After that, I would go almost immediately to Sergio Leone, the Italian director with those spaghetti Westerns. He's like the equal of the Greeks. But, since he's Italian, he should be.

Q. In addition to the figure of the cowboy in these essays, there's a second Western character—the figure of the city man. You say the most interesting Westerner was always a city man.

Isn't there a kind of Westerner who gets away with being a city man because people in the West don't really know what a city man is? You know, that city-slicker image?

A. Oh, the New England captain, like Gregory Peck, who goes to Texas?

Q. In the first lines of *Gunslinger*, there's this figure with impeccable smoothness, hands encased in leather—a stylish figure, who has the kind of self-conferred aristocracy of the city-bred character, but whose credentials are only that he acts that way. He could have just got out of jail, for all anybody knows. He doesn't have to show his transcript from Harvard.

A. The gambler, absolutely. The gambler and the gunfighter in the West are the Khomeinis of the West. Definitely. All you have to do is translate into Western terms—the "canon" is the gun, the "dictum" is the gun. Sure. The reason I'm trying to call people's attention to the concept of absolutism in terms of style is precisely because of that. There's no *content* to any of this, really. I mean if you read Khomeini's content, you're going to read that you have to start by washing the back of your neck, and then you proceed to your right ribs, and then you go to your left, and then you wash your hands, and then you go on down and so forth. And no matter how clean you get yourself, it's still *invalid* if you haven't done it that way.

Q. But isn't absolutism a very aristocratic style at all times? Like the British army, never apologize, never explain. It's bred into the tradition of aristocratic behavior, an absolutism of style?

A. No, the way I read that is, style is whatever is admired. And for better or worse, that's the whole point of democracy—that it demands style. When it *doesn't,* then it's getting sold cheap. When it's got lame leaders who can't talk, like we've got now. That's not my kind of democracy. That's its low point. Literally, that lack of style. And what you must remember, also, which is politically terribly important, is that this nation didn't start as a democracy. It wasn't called that for quite a few years. In the first place it was called mobocracy. And that was during the period when they burned houses down. But the *main* activity was tearing them apart. The guys who did that were the wreckers. The house-wreckers. If they didn't agree with some guy's opinion, they'd go around one night—it was the opposite of the shivaree. It happened in Philadelphia a lot, like if an idea people didn't like appeared in the newspaper—Philip Freneau, who's said to be the first American poet—he was a lousy poet, but he was also the first great American journalist—was the editor of the Philadelphia newspaper. It was Jefferson's newspaper. The people who worked for that newspaper got their houses wrecked a lot. And we're talking about two-story frame houses, with a lot of wood—they were big houses. A mob of 200 people would come around with crowbars and hammers, and they'd just take the house apart. They'd smash up the furniture. What you'd have left after that is these total splinters that used to be a house.

Q. So that is part of the growing pains of the concept of the individual as applied to politics?

A. Well, it's true, this is—I don't hear it said much any more, but it used to be said a lot, in fact it was our primary excuse— that we're a young country, right? We've aged so rapidly recently that nobody's saying it much any more, but in fact it's still true. The other thing is that nobody can wait for history any more. So for instance a nation as young as we are wouldn't even have been noticed formerly when nations took longer to be birthed. But now when everything's supposed to happen so quickly, 200 years is just—like everybody's impatient with it. And it's nothing. But we should have at least a thousand years, for us to even be talked about. I mean it was formerly true. And now we're the big exception.

Q. Don't you think, speaking of democracy and political structure, that the big function of the writer is to do what these guys 200 years ago were getting their houses burned down for, that is, to resist? Somewhere close to the nerve of democracy, a useful function for resistant expression seems to be built in. The angularity of just taking a position that's not being taken, because it's individual, and running it down and trying it—if that function were more active in democracy, if more writing were done from a resistant point of view, it might have a healthy effect on policy and on the nation.

A. I agree completely. In fact, it was always held that democracy couldn't be healthy or even exist without contention. Contention is what democracy most needs. Now there's no contention.

Q. In the eighteenth century, from which the ideas behind our political structure derive, didn't literary contention often breed a higher degree of focus and perception? It seems that we've lost that—

A. Completely. People were willing to insult each other in that century. All the time. It was a total century of insult. And it was a brilliant century. It invented the modern. And you can tell by looking at what people had to say to each other that it had such hope for the modern. And remember, it had already laid the foundation of modern science. It had given it its technique. I mean it was the real break. Neo-classicism was the real break with what had come up to us. Obviously, its betting on the future was heavy, and it was very positive. I mean the fact that the future has totally disowned that, and failed it, is no comment on the hope that was lodged in that century. I mean, it's now looked back on as unsanitary. It's now looked back on as arch, in this kind of pernicious way. For one thing, Enlightenment has now become the false hope of the East. What was meant by Enlightenment in the West was far too bright for anybody to actually buy who wasn't actually in the West. The hope was too great. It literally represented the moon. I mean, that's the scientific part of it. And now it's possible that a lot of people are trying to sell us a bill of goods that's not the hope. When diminished expectations are sold as a commodity, you get Governor Brown and Linda Ronstadt. With nothin' in between.

Q. You say in your essay on Douglas Woolf that to move West too young can sour a man's wit. Do you think that happened to you?

A. No I don't, because I arrived in the West rather late. When I was in high school, my first trips were *through* the West. I was going to California, which isn't the West. That's Pacific. The West became my laboratory. And it's the subject I'm most interested in. But I was never subject to that danger, precisely *because* I was able to warn anybody who took it up. When I was in high school, taking my trips across the country on a Trailways bus, or in cars, in that old car pool that used to exist. You know, pay $20 and go to L.A. You'd have six people and you'd drive all the way through. I was going to California, to Seal Beach. I feel much more Californian than Western in that way, I always have. I was going to California when I was 16 years old. I was brought up a nomad.

Q. Do you think you'll go on being a nomad?

A. There's an awful lot of pressure now to stop all that. And in fact the numbers are getting extremely more and more coercive against movement at all. Movement, thought, anything—

the numbers are coercing against it. They're entering the machines. Soon the power of the machines is going to be overwhelming. The machines' capability is already great, but the data is deficient. But once the data catches up with the capability, it's going to be more and more difficult to move, anywhere. So we're seeing the last years of all we're talking about. The mind that represents movement is going to have to think of a whole different set of configurations to perpetuate itself. The ways it has perpetuated itself are coming to an end. The rise in price of airplane tickets is a good indication. The fact that the railroad is being sold as safer, more meditative, more ecological, a lot slower—but no cheaper—is an indication of it. All you have to do is increase all that to get total stoppage.

Statement for
the Paterson Society

My poems usually deal with things that are difficult for me to arrive at by any other means than the poem. They are remote from me, not in their proximity always, but in their difficulty. They are rarely "domestic" because that is not my natural expression. I never think of what I write as important to anyone else, that is, I never make that requirement. I have no desire at all to rule other people's necessity for my own involvement. If I read my poems publicly, which I propose to do shortly, it is because I would like to and because I imagine some people might enjoy listening to me read. I have no illusions whatsoever about people at large being in need of poets or their work. It is demonstrated daily that they have their own business, and very little time for anything else unless it is something which will enable them to while away in some measure of peace or interest what remains to them. Poetry is never a means of relaxation. If it becomes that it dies immediately, in the hands of the reader.

Nor do I consider poems the means of other than private

statement. Content may be anything at all. Culture is based on what men remember, not what they do, fortunately. Even a civilized man who can read and write will occasionally exhibit this memory, at which times it is said of a man he acted with loveliness. If the poet is to make a more cognizant reality the poetry must be a self-occupying art. There are hardly any materials to stand in the way. Great preoccupation may, given other necessities, make great poems.

In the above sense it can be interesting for listeners to determine for themselves if a poet has written his own poems or merely "practiced" perseveringly, in the literature.

Santa Fe, New Mexico
December 6, 1960

What I See
in *The Maximus Poems*

PART I: THERE ARE PLACES

There are a handful of places in America today where artists
gather, in all their varieties, and some of them, New York,
San Francisco, are large cities, with all the commitments to
that size, i.e., streets that are busy over most of the day, traf-
fic problems, buildings filled with other people, and generally,
the so-called frenzy of specially concentrated peoples. Suburbs
where it is said really important people like computers live,
and so on. Other towns, Santa Fe, Taos, Aspen, perhaps a
place or two in Missouri, and the ones in New England, are
much smaller, the buildings, streets, parties, private libraries
and public, don't come on so fabulously. It is dangerous to
imply that artists are either numerous or plentiful, no matter
how true it is they are widespread. This doesn't at all depend
on what one's *taste* is.

I find myself in one such particular place. Right now,
this evening, there are some very nice bells coming from

Christo Rey. Across the Santa Fe River. Perhaps a half-mile away. The sound fading into groves of cottonwood. There are departures like this that belie all the other grossnesses of this town, and for a brief period the sense is changed, and you feel as it is possible to feel about Santa Fe, not as the various literatures tell you you should. One really *is* in New Mexico. One really *is* 7000 feet high. The threading Rio Grande really *is* off to the right, though many miles, down through what is to this day, a desolate and very breathtaking country. But the sweep-out of that land one can see standing here, where it runs down all the way more and more barren, away from the pine breaks of the mountains, to a moon-land, to Albuquerque, and below. And then at this time once in a while, I walk up to the ridge back of the house and can see the most standing thing on any of the horizons: the bulwark of the Sandias which is opposite Albuquerque. Or as Meline said, Albuquerque lies at the foot of . . . 60 miles south. For all of its clearness, visibility, the sky itself is variation, accompanying the landscape.

Artists and skies, the range of the Sandias, later, the Indians and a few other things. This is perhaps a harsh way to talk, throwing the components of this place together, human and nonhuman, all together in the same bag. I certainly don't do this because I am impelled toward that basis from a wish to be modern and cold, "dehumanized." Not at all. In those terms, I know what I am doing. The reason is: it is not in my hands to do otherwise. As everyone knows, places vary widely. In spite of the fact the earth is reputed to be a ball, the formality stops there. And that man is of one species and can interbreed, endlessly, is not the same thing. Man makes his true hybrids manifest in the acts of men. Ultimately the general mass of men act the same from a desire, but as you come up, there is a smaller way of looking at it. For instance, Kemerer is not the same as Santa Fe, which is not the same

as Biloxi. But all men try to act the same, there is the generality. "Nature is less indulgent. After the mule comes nothing,"
said Gauguin.

So that place has to shift for itself, largely. It is all *there,*
certainly, and presumably, always was, but that isn't enough.
Man, who is distinct from nature, will attempt almost anything. This has, unfortunately, a limited interest for the rest
of us. Because, though the direction, even stated intent, may
differ, be a nuance, the place he comes back to, to show the
rest of us, the spot as a motivation, his very maligning reason,
does not change, it officially is always the same. And when he
takes off from the green and grey earth, from wherever, Kemerer or Santa Fe, he returns with the news, not surprising,
that the planets are inhabited by the same creatures he is,
with the same propensities for the half-cocked, the same deception in his well-stated motives. Finds, and brings back
specimens we are already shy of, alas. But the trip out was
ostentatious. That is not rewarding, either. Because place, as
a nonhuman reality, is simply outside the presentments of
human meaning. And not interesting. Although sometimes it
may be. But I doubt it.

No. Where the depth, the strata are, that we as human
beings require it, to be satisfied with the revelation, the re-
curring nouns that pronounce our lives, these are wilder
places, not cast indefinitely upon the earth any more than
gold is. Prose flounders now because it seeks to celebrate
indiscriminately, out of a need for relief (we have gotten so
far from catharsis the word can't be used), but the relief
doesn't come on a continuing plane, and it is rather pitiful
to see its aspects of commentary dwindle to the size of sociologist apprehensions. Invention is not the point. That Indians
and artists and the mountains are the same here as the merchants, the artists and the mountains, all lying in the strata of
promotion I would never argue with. Because, having a flag-

ging patience, I won't bring forth something which balks at coming. Not that it depends on me and my ability. It is that I refuse to be a party to any sort of obscurity.

Places, the geographic and oceanic tidal surgings which have been common ground for man since time, are built, not rebuilt (that refers to ruins, for which there is no hope) or they are birthed again. There is no loss implied although I can't seem to shake a term that implies *second* or *following* . . . . Anyway a beautiful thing is occurring in America, today. By the way, I don't use the term Place as a mannerism, as an indiscriminate word, covering the "doings of man," at all. Not in any of the senses of the usability of anything, there is no functionalism meant, we mustn't have anything to do with arrangements put into people's hands, with reports or accounts, at the same time not discounting it is a Place, where the din, of everything that happened there, and is, comes to the ear, and eye, the building front, the woman's smile influenced by the school she attended etc., but that man standing at the side of the street shouting in Navajo, at the police cars, shaking his fist, going back and forth in a frenzy across the plaza to stand there, shaking his fist, screaming in abrupt Navajo, at the passing cars.

The beautiful thing is the writing now of *The Maximus Poems.* This is all that I am saying Santa Fe would only hypocritically yield. I.e., one could force it out, carry it farther than Vestal would, but it would be a trick, and interesting as that might be, it wouldn't at all serve to spring immensities of reality, of art, because they were never here. I am aware that at any time such a statement can be "disproven." Men came into this area governed on the one hand by what they distinctly found—Indians & raw space in front of them, and carrying, a principle—Spanish Christianity, which produced at most some interesting carved doors and Santos. That's about it. That isn't good enough to support a structure of place.

Indeed it propagates a condition for the effete, not the human art; the latter is dreadfully more deep and wide than the first. That is precisely why you found that the archaeologist, the anthropologist and the sociologist, take them all as one, flocked here. There was from the start a superabundance of the effete condition, surface, large thin space, and a principle just dead enough and known enough to make a likeable and easy complication in what they found. Which was *things,* which are effete. This is not a generality. It is awfully particular, it takes a very exacting registration, such as *Maximus* is capable of, to make *things* not effete, effects. The same thing, superficiality, probably explains too why opera is so popular here. And at the same time a predicament. Everyone wants an Art. But they want it too easily and casually, and they subscribe to very spurious people to get it sometimes. There is a series of letters in the local newspaper disputing the quality of reviews of the Opera. Naturally, when the local newspaper proceeded on its own account, for the first two or three performances it handled the thing as a social occasion. Which I comply with—opera has no possibility of art, it *is* a social occasion. But the ringer came when cultured people recognized this as a poor reflection on the *Place,* hence themselves, since they make up a disproportionate number. They wanted critical reviews, strictures, saying in effect, that this or that was or was not so, etc., treating the thing seriously, analyzing, cribbing the procedures of art. Of course it is indisputable that these people are art lovers. But what is that? This is the point: you don't have a place just because you barge in on it as a literal physical reality, or want it to prosper because you live there. Instead go see the Grand Canyon, that's what it was made for. Place, you have to have a man bring it to you. You are *casual.* This is a really serious business, and *not* to be tampered with. You might just as well live in Buenos Aires or Newfoundland, it doesn't make a damn bit of difference. But being casual, you have to be patient and intelligent.

Now, once we have got our place, or hope for it, the fine relieving quality and discrimination, Gloucester, the thing is then art, and you can never go to it, by any other route. It is the complex instrument I at least never cease to carry with me and be kept alive by, live under, and feel myself very damn glad to be on this lovely earth, having been given this gift. This is probably the only sense in which I am a child. It seems to me the way Homer must have worked. Not to be underneath the writing, not to have to pay attention to that. Olson is a master in the normal sense, i.e., there is no trafficking possible with his means, so tied to the source is he with his art. Nor can we learn anything of use from him. When other poets, those who exchange terms, whose mechanisms in a sense overlap, or make sense in a functional procedural way to one another, address him "for Charles Olson" it isn't necessarily improper, who is to say that, but it is beautifully senseless. As a man he is in Gloucester, that is definitely something else. One takes uses from minor writers. This is their availability and to some extent their value; they are not deeply tied and the display of their talent is thinly spread, covered with bubbles, temporarily available to the eyes. They come to realizations late, and as an afterthought to their art. Wilde is an example. They never resurrect, theirs is a technology of the senses. It isn't that Olson doesn't manifest the same recognizable properties that mark writing. It is that the terms are not extractable from the whole art: there are no terms, but there is the term of the form. It isn't just a piece of logic to say that for the total art of Place to exist there has to be this coherent form, the range of implication isn't even calculable. I know *master* is a largish word. I don't mean my master. I mean Dostoevsky, Euripides. The power. It is a removal from the effete and at the same time the aesthetic. There was a certain fascism (not the political term) that existed in american writing for the last 35 years or more or less, in which the zeal for material effect was the cardinal quality, material effect being something that impresses itself by virtue of itself, per se, in which the springing is neither inward nor outward, but merely within. Images suffer. Techné is brought in.

Well, that is ended now, even though it is still practiced. Here in Santa Fe. The indians are down in the plaza, some of them probably don't have a way home, but there seem to be many pickup trucks. My man is probably there too, screaming in his off-reservation world. Haniel Long has been dead three years. Somewhere out there, I don't know where the cemetery is, the wind is blowing over his grave, blowing the grass and weeds, I must find out where he is buried.

Long was the only man concerned himself with art, here in the place, concerned with place. He never had one. He is a minor writer. A great minor writer, in America, and he had the radical mind it takes for that kind of art. He was involved with aesthetics, like minor art is, because the components themselves, the members that come together to make their art are always on the outside, as though the building were reversed in its construction, showing its structure first, enclosing its content, interiorly and arbitrarily. For want of the aspects of total place. The elements he brings forward would normally be those given elements that gracefully go together in an accordance which one could retain the mystery and buoyancy of and thus have the timelessness of the effect, which is what is lingering, and knows no tenses, the now, the then, the will be. Cabeza de Vaca and Haniel Long. And, his wandering Christ figure, who traversed the Southwest barefoot from Denver to the border, and cured, cast lovely spells, who had long hair, was a man full of grace and humility, a violent kind, who talked too much, walked, was lonely, and had meaning and cognizance, was followed, there was an awe. Would normally have been his elements, had, as I say, there been a concordance of place for him to work, but reality is not manysided like a prism here, here geology is, and the excavations will never cease. It was no loss to him probably. I love Long's writing for this abstraction of fulfillment. It *was* a loss to us. *Piñon Country* is the specimen of a radical mind with no home, no anchorage; as artist this is the one factor outside our control.

But when the Place is brought forward fully in form conceived entirely by the activation of a man who is under its spell it is a resurrection for us and the investigation even is not extractable. And it is then the only *real* thing. I am certain, without ever having been there, I would be bored to sickness walking through Gloucester. Buildings as such are not important. The wash of the sea is not interesting in itself, that is luxuria, a degrading thing, people as they stand, must be created, it doesn't matter at all they have reflexes of their own, they are casual, they do more than you could hope to know, it is useful, it is a part of industry. It has an arrogance of intention. This is the significance of Olson's distrust of Thucydides and his care for Herodotus. It is the significance of Blake's "the practice of art is anti-christ." Which further means that if you are not capable of the nonfunctional striking of a World, you are not practicing art. Description, letting things lay, was reserved for not necessarily the doubtful, but the slothful, or the merely busy.

> The places still
> half-dark, mud,
> coal-dust.
>
> There is no light
> east
> of the bridge
>
> Only on the headland

toward the harbor
from Cressy's

have I seen it (once
when my daughter ran
out on a spit of sand

isn't even there). Where
is Bristow? when does I-A
get me home? I am caught

in Gloucester. (What's buried
behind Lufkin's
Diner? Who is

Frank Moore?

—"The Librarian"

This is toward the most acute possible measurement. All
the arrogance of intention that pervades Place is left out of
"The Librarian" poem. The beginning of the poem, right down
through the first two stanzas, is the key to this code of location, as of now. We can come home. From the Pacific or out
west. And the ending fragment beginning, "The places still
. . . ," is my reunion with the nouns and questionings, of my
life, it makes me weep, there is no loss suffered, I am very
much excited, what next, who is Frank Moore? When does
I-A get me home?

The singular problem is difficult to come at. There is
no contention that things, in the sense that one holds them,
material things, but that is rather limiting, because utensils
aren't only meant, or santos, or carved doors, or the "I" and
all its predicament, its environment, inclement and unhappy,
and in general the ranges upon ranges of materially disposed
things that contain the mines of our lives, there is no conten-

tion that these things are really permanently deadening to us, they *are* grotesque in their deathly confrontation. I am perhaps a little suspicious about their strength, but that's all right. The important thing is that the only quarantine we have from them now is this new discovery of a total disposition of them in the human inherited sense. Coming all at once, and large, it is a morphology that up to now has been lacking. There is no aesthetic to bring us back into a social world of intention, delaying by way of modern functionalism our grasp, shortening our vision, putting us back outside again, where we spend so much time traveling the hall of distraction and apportionment, not ever coming to rest in cognizance and lingering mystery. Mystery, as it stands, is not a good word to apply to *Maximus,* because what I see in *The Maximus Poems* is the compelling casting of light over the compounds that make it up. I.e., regardless of their own distinct natures. There is a gain for me since there is nothing I detest so much as objectivity. So my sense of the mystery is: awelike, something unknown but more importantly, cognizant, a crest, by which our common histories are made human again, and thrilling, for *no* other motive than they are ours.

PART II: HOW THE TWO PARTS OF THE
WORLD DO NOT COME TOGETHER.

The minute anything is illustrated for me, a point, a religion, a doctrine, etc., I immediately lose interest. Any validities I am able to pick up, I pick up through my own peculiar senses, and I must say it took me long enough to become sufficiently bored with understanding and reason, to abandon them altogether. Haniel Long said, "The nucleus of free People is a matter so delicate that I wonder if we can ever see it except through the eyes of the spirit." Well, I am not considering people so much as I am everything I meet.

It is one of the lovely qualities of Western Man that he is abstract. What I mean by abstract is, as far purely away from nature as he can get, thus bringing into fruition all the properties of man, simply. This same abstraction is the background for his intense ugliness too, and generates such men as scientists, and the men who hire them. It seems a necessary dual. When the Oriental Philosophy scholar uses as an illustration of the "difference between east and west" the construction of a paper flower, taking the petals and stamen from a box and placing them on a wire stem, with his sickening laborious smile, as an example of the way the west makes a flower, Materialism, Process, Power, Arbitrary, you see, Dominion, removing the components from a box and arranging them by Will, as, say, against, the other illustration, now to come in which the flower (the same damn paper flower by the way, always) grows: this is a photographic trick (which is still the west, because that's where the lecture occurs) but in spite of your eyes, this is the flower growing, unfolding itself before your very eyes gents, and it is cynical to see the transfer for what it is and not very kind to the current propaganda for the east. With its tradition of multiple armed gods. But Materialism, Power, Dominion etc. are the ischial callosities (those things that hang down on an orangutan) of the West which are promptly kicked by anyone anywhere who has even a pretense of education.

I imagine some people do believe that in the one example the flower is built out of the force of the "ego" of Western man ("who never lets anything lay") and that in the other the flower really does grow all by itself, a kind of immaculate conception of the universe. Well, whatever happens in immaculate conceptions, I don't trust the universe. I would kick it in the teeth if it came near me. Because I have thus far seen the universe to be in the hands of such men who would parry such examples. Of course it isn't to be imagined that *anyone* is talking about the stars. No, no. This is for much bigger game, the winning and welding, the cohesion of men's souls. The stars are fixed, more or less, already. Whatever the benign outward gesture, only the individual (I don't mean the word in the old doctrinal sense of a way to be a liberal, but as "anyone") has the carrying power of the soul and its responsibilities of the community, also those historical. The consequence of all this is that I don't find the "ego" at all obnoxious, but am aware it is an undesirable word now; what I want though is its centrality. There are other words perhaps less committed one could use in talking of what goes on in *The Maximus Poems*. Enough qualification to say I am not using it as a personal limitation, nor in its political senses. It reverts to my insistence that a creation of the order of *Maximus* comes exclusively from a man, and if dependencies are evident, it is the man we go to for their explication, not the so-called source. But the ego has been dangerous only since Freud defiled it at the same time he saved puritanism, after the latter had nearly died in the nineteenth century: by simply and deftly shifting the field of taboo from the body to the mind. Fortunately though, there's no harm done, because the reality and the art remain the same, "only man can make a tree" . . . God's business is subject to mood, and wars with the times.

If I am irrelevant to bring in the ego, you will correct me. But this is what I fully mean: No matter how much I may want ego to be a centrality, it is practically worthless as "center." In the senses of self and center the ego lacks meaning, and this class of senses disintegrates immediately into something cheap and commercial and psychiatric. A center existing within any periphery is simple enough. It is a bore. Its location is a little more interesting but only utilitarianly so, and that, as a pursuit, is a chief method of keeping clever people busy. The technology of the senses. Taking the ear as preparatory opposite of speech, I suppose it plays its part in necessity, but it disturbs me, and I would never give that organ a place other than as a deviant, much like a messenger, who goes about among the princely senses, carrying data which is very often drab in its accuracy and practicality. "I couldn't believe my ears." And seldom do.

There is a term of ego in *Maximus,* and although I know it as a general thing it branches from specific places. Melville: *Redburn:* What Redburn saw in Launcelott's-Hey: "It's none of my business, Jack. I don't belong to that street." "Who does then?" "I don't know. But what business is it of yours? Are you not a Yankee?" "Yes," said I, "But come, I will help you remove that woman, if you say so." This could be reduced to nothing more than a "personal concern" but what would be the value of such a point as that? I prefer it in the light of one of the minor workings of Melville's ego, which in other places roamed a much wider pasture. In some senses it is a method, but again that's not what I am taking it as. Rather the great vivid homage, placing a zebra amongst elk, banding with elk. Not as a value concerning either elk or zebra. But as a placement on this earth, as an environment in which things are pronounced; otherwise, I suppose everyone is familiar with the defense of uniformity and placid reason.

And if there is a "good" for mankind as a whole it is in just such an isolation that he gains it for the whole, not, as the decipherers of the problem of how to bring the two halves of the world together, "East & West," would have us believe, that we will gain the whole more directly by forsaking Will and Ego, first, become a window through which things, a channel, etc. It isn't so bad that men wish to dominate us, because in a cliché they do anyway, but the realm of thought that seeks to make it "natural" is what I cry out against. Granted that men have a beautiful oceanic sense of their predicament, and that it is common, and that this very sense rests absolutely on the existence of the thing that separates him from and makes him more than the equal of nature (not in the active sense of course, but it is a recent discovery that he must match an earthquake to make his point) there is a terrifying proposition that he abandon the only thing he has with the promise that he later will regain it, even better. And in the interim, when he has his guard down? What will happen? You know goddamn well what will happen, he will never see himself again, but will see the universe or some other ice-cream cone, and then when he is most down they will slip him a bowl of *merde* about having eight arms, and three faces. As if this, finally, isn't a beastly limitation anyway!

Which is enough to say the ego is a dangerous thing. I can't see that Whitman did anything but degenerate it again with his line. I mean in his line. The line is not distinctly responsible for what happened. Its peculiar length and sway is not the working of what is real and birth-giving, the nonargumentative edification of human event. Rather it is the helpless output length of an ego which wasn't practically able to terminate itself in a relationship with nature, so that his participation, his own determinant lagged always before the onslaught of the so-called outside world. It seems an odd time to trot Whitman in. His value is the study of the expansion of the ego. I don't know when ego became personal, but it was an unfortunate thing. But probably it was *made* personal. And that fencing produces only expansion. Expansion has a way of instantly becoming an echo, and is compulsive like Echo. The scream makes its point the first time, which is all right, but it then by rudeness abolishes the recurrence in the mind, which factor is, in fact, about the only thing one has left, granted we are alive. Which is to say, the energy of beauty consumes itself. This is not a valuable suicide.

I know of only two kinds of historic gods. The first are seemingly spontaneous men who appear on the earth and are rather direct in their talents, more or less wise in their ways. And the touching thing about them is that we love them very much and they are figures of great suffering, sympathy and tenderness. And something political happens to them, or they become the property of political intrigue, for civil jurisdiction, then, for centuries. Christ is the most prominent victim, the most prominent of this kind of god. The other kind of god isn't political at all necessarily. But he might be incidentally, and it isn't his suffering that is so important about him. And it is impossible to use him as a force of deception because his clarity rests in beauty. And he remains unexploited in his existence in us, because he is abstract and illustrates nothing tending to be lowly. Hector. He could not be farther from the example of the flower, because again, flowers mean nothing to man except his own flowers, those he has brought forth, and he loves them as does nature love her flowers. This isn't to say he also can't love nature's flowers. A poet created Hector. In a sense Christ wasn't created. This made possible his resurrection, and the resurrection harks back to the immaculate nonhuman conception. Hector is not resurrectable. He lives in the manor of the mind and stands for unalienated beauty. And certainly man has a nature in that sense. Hector died in battle with the natural ugliness of the world, symbolized as the state in the form of Achilles. The death was final. And the abstraction this event drifted to is the pure abstract. Which is to say it is free from the commitments life in general, life in the Everyday, life in its mechanics, has made. Christ is hopelessly involved in the secrets of the State, because his ego was perverted for its use. Hector still possesses a free ego, the kind of circuit which stays in the human breast in the form of beauty (even such a thing as behavior was once beauty), but the ego, as well as beauty, and things abstract, are pagan. Whereas Christ was quickly utilized out of existence, Hector remained, precisely because he wasn't chosen. The chosen is the blackest fate of all, and that's why my heart still yearns over Christ. The Roman world rose on the shoulders of a god which is cut on the secular pattern, because beauty is isolated and abstract, while virtue and grace are infinitely manipulatable. *Maximus* returns to a pre-Christian ordering of the ego, or however, comes forward to a non-Christian ordering—thus journeying out to prepare the day for a new look at man, from a spirit which has an unerring knowledge of what is decent and lovely and dignified in man.

It would be too much to say that all this is being offered as a strict knowledge of anything. It, needless to say, has a validity only in the sense that it is the quick casting of the world I am in as I look at *Maximus.*

PART III: A LOOK AT THE POEMS:
A NONTECHNICAL NOTE

Actually, I'm not going to look at the poems because I already have, many times. There is no point in talking about the way they are put together, in a subtotal sense, because, in the first place, I never had a taste for analysis, and in so far as technique goes, there is Olson's projective verse essay, and besides, any man ought to do that work for himself. Offhand I would say the best single poem to go to to test his own statements about verse is "On first Looking out through Juan de la Cosa's Eyes." I say this to mean it has more exactly the particular turnings, springs, shutters, the weavings, and the riding away, that I take it this verse has when it works best. But picking out that one poem is not the point either, because I at least find a consistency of success which will enable you to go anywhere to find what might be the very best of the whole. Which is just great. Because I read, to use an opposite, I read spontaneously. I.e., I am probably interested in the language at all times, just because I am. I don't particularly care the

way it is arranged. I like the way it is, on the page, and find
great sense in the way it is, and relevantly, in the way Olson
says it ought to be. But I don't depend on it. In one sense, I
am completely anticritical. But maybe I mean not critical at
all. The distinction of whether a thing is verse or poetry or indeed prose bores me. I hate the term *verse,* though. Which
seems to me so small and clerkish and embarrassed in the face
of Poetry. Poetry is currently put squeamishly down as a
term, as though we are all embarrassed and afraid of our own
knowledges about what it is and what it is not. To me, by
their ring, there is no misunderstanding of such familiar terms.
They have no meaning in a literal sense, you always mean
them emotionally anyway, and if this is the case I unabashed-
ly say, Poetry. But I, for a niceness, take "The Twist" as the
highest achievement of *The Maximus Poems,* prior to "The
Librarian" (which I understand is not, strictly speaking, a *Maximus* poem). And the low quarter exists for me in the first
line of all: "By ear, he sd/." This is not a fussing of the given
dogma, because I will leave alone what is necessary for Olson.
To me it is simply a false preamble to a work which I feel
vastly, and subsequently doesn't comprise the remaining sub-
stance of the poem. I bring it up only because it is a tenet,
and as held, the poem takes its rising from there. And breaks
out of that conch wherein the sound merely, of the sea is
heard, along about "The Song and Dance of," which is the
stage setting for "The Twist," to come, and by that time is
definitely off the singular pole of Ear. I say this not because
I notice a clicking change of metrics, or anything that neat.
But because I sense a turning of the human attitude. Already
in "Juan de la Cosa."

And in "The Twist" is the seed sown from which springs
"The Librarian," and if I am correct, what is now to come. The
nouns seem to calm themselves first here, and take on the
sheerings and simplicity of immediate knowledge which re-

sides together in what is more felt, the searching substantives of the inscribed field of Gloucester. Are the measure of where we are always. It has a nice closeness. The compounds, Olson and me, or whoever. Beginning "Trolley-cars/ are my inland waters" the compound is spoken quite distinctly as in the first person: "Or he and I distinguish/" "It rained,/ the day we arrived." "She was staying,/ after she left me," "When I found her" "When I woke." And then follows the two beautiful letters 19 and 20, with the same attendant breathing of the first person nominative, out into reality, "the opening out/ of my countree." And this generosity is essentially different, these pronoun beginnings, than the more or less quick benevolence of "you sing, you/who also/wants." Anyway, it must be obvious, it is the matrix which interests me rather than the metrics.

[Santa Fe, 1960]

New York, New York

(It's a wonderful place to live but a poor place to visit)

It seems like that cliché got backwards. Once clichés get
turned around, sometimes they become the truth again. Test-
ing others of like density, there isn't much doubt. I never
lived there, so I am certain I've never been there.

Like other "provincial" places (and *all* places are) there
are certain things make one laugh, for instance, middle-class
people say things like "Oh, that's some more of that middle-
class horseshit." Which is equitable enough. Not exactly to be
called seeing through yourself, yet it's a nice laziness. In the
outlands often the populace is so energetic it won't say it.

I didn't notice much because I kept my eyes on people's
faces, what I went to look at. I didn't get to *know* a single
soul I hadn't already known for years. I *met* several and that
was fine, I can say without qualification. The numbers of people, although they are a famous entity, and one could count
them, someone must have, aren't really the point, or one
hardly sees them. A very civilized arrangement. No not civi-

lized, necessary. Riding on the subway once we got caught, I heard because of a fire. And no one moved even an eyelash. This seemed to me not so much a sign of deadness, of shells, but something better than making noise and thrashing the arms. In the non-New York part of the country which stretches for a few thousand miles to the West, people are so sentimental about *Space* they would scream, although it would come out a long ear-splitting drawl, if so confined, if so logically stopped. One shouldn't go right on through fires unless you are getting paid for it. That seems reasonable. And then when we surfaced, the taxis didn't want to pick us up, and that seemed reasonable too, who were we? They knew who they were, and they were going elsewhere.

When we were going we passed through Chicago, which is familiar enough, my mother and some other relatives I hadn't seen for a long time came up from the South to see us; we were three hours between trains. Chicago has that rural ring certainly, although one will see a few semi-elegant men walking down the streets in raincoats of the proper luster and length. Very obvious imports. Everything seems natural in New York, i.e., there isn't that necessity to figure out the origins of people and things there is in an arbitrary town like Chi. Wynd. L. said NY was a business center and nothing else, really. That it must be, and nothing else. *The* business, of reviewing people, screwing people, spewing on people, and dumping them in the harbor or giving them a ticket to get the hell to Weehawken. One hopes, i.e., I am sanguine it is too much for chambers of commerce, but it probably isn't. The real heroes are the mob, and their twin, the fuzz, and nobody is angry in any important sense they can't be paid for, or haven't gone there, which to become. In the sense that it is raw it must be very like the garden of Eden, *before* Snake, Blind. They see only when they want an apple. When a man lies puking his TB guts up in the gutter he's not an apple, and that could hardly be refuted with conventional reasoning. That kind of honesty is rather thin, one might think at first, but what, one finds always, gets thick, is dishonesty. But the opposition isn't always very engaging. I do agree with Barry Goldwater that the Eastern seaboard should be cut loose from the rest of the country, set adrift. Of course for exactly contrary reasons.

New York is the colony that didn't fail, like New Harmony, Indiana did. I like it in that limited sense because there are people who don't belong there, being there for reasons I wasn't quite able to make out, oh I made out all the logical ones, but I think a lot of people must live there because they can get good egg-creams. That's for the people who live there, but most of them don't, but that's something else and I gather need not be considered at all.

There is more advantage to it (NY) than meets the eye, I'd bet. Even a poor man could be exclusive there. This is a way of being that even a poor man ought to have open to him if he wants it. In a small outland town if you don't take a certain street, sooner or later you'll live to regret it. In large spaces, with small amounts of people one much sooner gets hung up literally with physical impediments. Fences, corners, walls, posts, curbs, tanks, barrels, you could extend the list, for hours. Given space it must be cluttered in one way or another. In NY I noticed the cars were mostly on the street, the people on the sidewalk, and the rather nicely proportioned and thick high buildings back of that. I was at a housing development once, this one was a middle-classed one, just an outland perversion of how to live, they had told them, and they had believed them and everyone bought it. That part of NY I would never go near if I lived there. And they aren't too important, any of the housing developments. After a while everyone will forget that horseshit and go back to nice crowded buildings all facing up and down a street, and live thickly, which is what New York is for, what it does that the outland can't, what it was meant to be, not by any idiot planner of course, but by the spirit naturally inherent in the terms of an island. On the other hand the problem of people having to live thickly when they don't choose it, is a simple one, and one that planning is impotent before—thieves and cutthroats like mobbers and bankers choose not for them to be, as they would choose. Therefore there is no choice. It is an interesting paradox that the most downtown part, the so-called financial district, is taken as quaint by otherwise ordinarily intelligent people. It is the only blighted spot on the island, and a cancer which exists for the nation in its outland totality. It is a grim, vicious, poisonous section and I never walked through it without a shudder of horror. Everyone must agree, with good reason. Mid-town is neither here, nor is it there, and can be ignored altogether, it is not, what it is commonly supposed to be, a dangerous stretch of the island. Those people there do as they are told, and rather promptly.

These are loose impromptu impressions. What I really liked was seeing people unexpectedly on the street I knew and love. It doesn't often happen that way out here, and not altogether principally because I don't love too many people here but more because there aren't enough people here. It's hard to get them to come. And why not? There's really nothing here except a lot of famous space and a little of that goes a long ha way. Whoopee. Everyone was nice there and that doesn't happen often that everyone for the most part is nice. It's nice. There is one thing that makes NY the most relaxed place I've not been in, and that's that everyone knows he's there, where everything probably is. Don't underestimate that. It means you can finally pull off your shoes and say OK let's stop walking, we're here. Not so much nasty talk about how and where to live, although if there is that it takes the form of an abstract obligation, as though they pay tribute to something they aren't really interested in, but because it is the human and agreeable thing to do. No unnecessary fights, the only time you scream is when you get your head caught in a subway train door (one of those old rusty ones), which I did. Although I didn't scream, not wanting to appear a hick. A great temptation though. But you can't and mustn't. Because then the whole thing becomes meaningless, and they would have to tell you—"OK, you did it, now you have to go." And that would be true, you'd have to go. Back West into all that neurasthenic space where I am not convinced yet a young man should go. It's OK if you're older and have your wits about you, but if you go there too young, and stay too long, your wit sours, or you can get rich by murdering the land you came to love, try to avoid the severance tax, try not to feel too out of it, become the chronic sayer of—"I get to NY once a year."

Out here, it's still of course that kind of a "rush," and for that reason I finally like the fact that new york city, the island, is for the most part covered over with concrete, it takes the mind off dirt, what's in it, under it, of it. Salute, it will always be a nice city so long as it doesn't become "pleasant" to visit. Or Pleasant to live in. That quality in a city if it becomes really established is bad. The people become obnoxiously egoistical, and nutty, they pat their tummies just to feel that fine fresh air moving into their silly gullets, they strike that green grass with the air of a pimp whose affairs are going nicely. San Francisco is one of those places. The other side of the coin. A word does for all of them—STOP.

The most that can be said of a city will be what is going on there, not necessarily intelligently—that's always too much to ask—but that there ought to be lots of whatever it is. The disposition of Space is pretty unimportant. That's mechanical, how far is it to the building, to the store, to the corner, to his house, to her breast, to his job. It is very mechanical and if not impossible, works. It has to work and does mostly, and if not, then becomes like the machine, very tedious if it doesn't work. People always work better than any arrangement they are able to make. One especially nice thing about New York is its shape, it is long rather than wide. This is the source of endless pleasure. Going up and down.

[Pocatello, 1961]

Nose from Newswhere

Early in May I returned from the middle west, back to the mountains. I had been abroad only two weeks, yet it seemed much longer than that; nights spent in strange places, still trying to get it all sorted and placed on some scale of impression. Several hours after I got off the train someone said, "Ammon is here." I said, oh, yes, and smiled. He hadn't been around here since last winter, had it been in January or December, just before Christmas?

Back then I had written a letter to him asking if he would come up for a few days, chew the fat, fast, anything. He said yes, so Ray and I drove down to pick him up. That was a good visit. He talked everything from Carlo Tresca to curing (some process that seemed a hybrid of Christian Science and Buddha). In Salt Lake, before we started back, we had a bowl of soup at his refuge for derelicts and transients— one rule: no drunks and no cops—actually, I don't think he has all that much against drunks—it's just that like cops, they break things and are hard to handle and Ammon is slight of build, getting on in years. But the soup—great fat turnips and spuds, almost whole carrots floating around in rich hot broth. Very good. Gets plenty cold in Salt Lake. Ammon, I understand, does not eat of his own soup, being a vegetarian, but it is typical of the man that he knows fat warms, however it may chill the moral fiber of some thinkers.

If you ever find yourself in Salt Lake—I mean I doubt that you'd ever find yourself there—nevertheless if you're hungry, that hunger could be satisfied by what the St. Joseph's Refuge & Joe Hill House of Hospitality, at Post Office Place, has to offer—a lot of the food he uses he got from the Mormons, but you can hardly tell it by the taste.

Which gets me to what I had in mind—that Ammon has a way of transforming everything. He says he is a one man revolution, something about personal goodness, etc. To a man of my generation, bred on no sense of revolution save that literary talk, this seems quaint—all revolution does, here and now—i.e., ultimately one has to wonder who it would be would get the train for what station. (To the Salt Lake station? to the Grand Central station? I thought all those people had wives and kids in the garage, or I mean have to stop by the dry cleaners to pick up their beards.)

I saw Hennacy for just about a half hour this last time, here in Pocatello. Talked very fast . . . he mentioned he'd been in Seattle to picket the fair. I said, oh yes, how was that? And he told me. And I said, well, but what was there to picket? And he said, well, the fair, the 21st Century. I said, yeah, oh, the 21st Century. He said, sure. I said, you mean . . . He said, yea, you know, science, space, bombs, etc. I said, wow! a whole goddamn century, imagine, picketing that! He smiled, pleased. I was pleased too, that I finally got it. That I finally broke through all that crap I've read for the past few months, stuck somewhere on one little fix over the ravages of television or the national narcissistic murdering in Algeria.

And that's the nose from newswhere. That this smiling man had just come through from Seattle where he'd picketed the entire 21st Century—one thinks of all those fat businessmen up there who are already raking it in with their trade fair, already gloating, so far ahead, they think, cashing in on the next century. Hmmmm.

[Pocatello, 1962]

The New Frontier

> . . . and on his right side . . . a man
> who looked as though he knew all
> about mortgages but wanted to
> tell someone about politics.
>
> From: *Wall to Wall*

I assume Douglas Woolf's *The Hypocritic Days* is out of print.
It was published in January 1955 at Palma de Mallorca by Robert Creeley. As far as I know this was Woolf's first published
novel. In some ways it is more elegant in its prose than *Fade
Out* (1959) or *Wall to Wall* (1962). There are fewer slanted
meanings in it and those that are there quite readily point
themselves in the familiar direction. In *The Hypocritic Days*
Woolf tells us, in a very winning manner, what we want to
know of the situation at hand. It is usually not taken as a
good thing to tell us what we want or expect to hear. But all
good to great work is devoted to just that exercise; otherwise,
of course, it would be useless to speak of *any* sort of audience,
or even any single reader.

Woolf invites speculation about himself and his material to perhaps a greater extent than most other present novelists. He is a New Yorker. *The Hypocritic Days* are in Los Angeles. Billy the Kid is perhaps the most famous city man of the West. Probably all the very interesting westerners were city men. Certainly they have had an eastern home. The East has a very important stake in the West. Whether or not these men like it is not the question. The forms of such a system of hypocrisy L.A. has to offer are grotesque because L.A. is colonial. The colony is necessarily an exaggeration. The experience of *The Hypocritic Days* is grounded in Charles Ashton. In the colony, forms wear on the single man to a greater extent than in the regions where those forms are settled. The forms are transmitted only by the individual, there is no "tradition," nothing to absorb shock. As reality becomes tangent to a single man thus it is engaging. Otherwise L.A. is an ordinary place, you've been there. Outwardly it only seems a little more boring and laborious than other spots. But in its rigid underframing it will assert itself on those who have "grown up" there.

Lloyd, the monstrous, crippled "genius" of the first novel, sits in his bed in his high-priced L.A. apartment and broods like God over the captured circle of his subjects: other teenagers who like himself have something missing. In his case everything is missing of the physical, mobile realities. All that is life is a weird, precocious brain, and the sexual apparatus, which is plenty to go on, of course. But it makes for his captives, who like to use his place as a temple to hide their own desires in, a moral problem finally when, showing a movie set up by Lloyd's father, the movie turns out to be that filthy visual fornication the Elks and Moose so love to watch at their regional gatherings. For Charles Ashton, the sensitive young man trying to find a way in life for himself, it is a shattering event. He was tricked into operating the machine and when the screams of "turn it off" came, he couldn't find the switch in the darkened room. His girl, screaming directly at him, leaves in disgust but later returns, sends him home and stays on with Lloyd. It ends on that tone, quite powerfully, and one has no sense of a cute "switch" ending, it is simply one of the intimidating occurrences, one of the "intimations" or "realities" that Woolf so much attends.

There is I suppose an invitation to compare *The Day of the Locust* with *The Hypocritic Days.* There is no point in that. The latter book is not a Hollywood novel, and Woolf is a much subtler writer than West. Nor is Woolf a satirist in the strict sense. That point will be got to later. There is very little of the direct relationship of the author and reader in *The Hypocritic Days,* and what little of it there is disappears almost completely in the subsequent two books. I will quote one notable passage to show that Woolf could have become another kind of writer if he had so chosen. One of the few commentary passages from his first book:

> Loneliness is like the common cold, a contagious disease which we catch in public places and suffer in privacy. We turn from a man's loneliness as instinctively as we turn from his sneeze, but his germ overtakes us easily. We carry it home and doctor it with old remedies, all patently useless: there is no known cure for loneliness. The best we can do is to give it to someone else. Just as soon as we observe our symptoms in another, our own become less severe. Now let him look for someone else to pass his to, for we have developed an immunity. In a week we'll be feeling fit again, and an old man will die of unknown cause in Buffalo.

This passage occurs just after Charles' visit to Lloyd Lippincott in the afternoon, before the party, and as he takes leave of Mr. Lippincott, Lloyd's father, the man who is to fix the machine to show the film that night, when all Charles will have to do is to flip a switch to turn it on. Charles looks forward to going to work with Lloyd on a script, at $100 a week. These are heavy ironies of course. But they are never in quite the focus I have alleged here. Jan, Charles' girl, is pregnant by Charles. She, earlier, at first learning of the new arrangement between Charles and Lloyd (which is a remarkably Hollywoodian name) takes it as sick of Charles to work for a "sick" boy. An independent girl, as she is presented, that independence becomes, or does it? the occasion of her finally going to bed with Lloyd. Out of all this suggestion there emerges the fact that Charles is the man, as is Twombly, and finally Claude Squires. Is Claude Squires a subsequent Charles? At any rate, it is always, in all three books, the occasion for an Odyssey.

• • •

The Odyssey. Of Woolf's work, satire is only one of the pointed elements. And even then, taking the dictionary as guide, irony is more the important rule for him. A dissembler of speech. But formally, Woolf's novel disposes itself as an odyssey. This gets settled in *Fade Out*. In that way *The Hypocritical Days* is a prologue to the later two novels. And as much as I admire the first novel, it is not the equal of the later two, but an author's first novel is always of special interest, as is never the case of a first poem, which is invariably an embarrassment. Form. Form is all in poetry, and it doesn't matter that that form is loose or tight in this case. No form no poetry. About the only formality you can get into the novel is geometry. Geometry is the only figuration important to the novel. The declaration of space is the single external aspect of a novel. Woolf's novels are linear. They run in a line and in the case of *Fade Out* that line is a long curve with hitches in it, as is Homer's work, and in the case of *Wall to Wall* it is a segmented line, not straight, but not steadily curved, with a hook at the end. The casual reader is perhaps never very aware of form in a novel, but if that ruling were not there the casual reader would be destroyed immediately. The novel is the only art form the "public" does not have to train itself to understand. The meaning of a public art.

• • •

The American West is the place men of our local civilization travel into in wide arcs to reconstruct the present version, of the Greek experience. Not Greek directly of course. American. But there is where you will find the Stranger so dear to our whole experience. That the fear of the stranger has superseded what was once the curiosity about him is of minor importance, it comes from the same original well. And in the American West are denizens. It is a cultural movement. The denizens of the East are a "product" of neo-realism. Painters mostly are concerned with them. It is a concern and a definition that comes directly from industrialization. The American West, still in our time, has nothing to do with industrialization. In his desire to get out of the tight limitation of prime metals the westerner has constructed all of the sham formalities of a world that has gone beyond that rawness. The witness of any city between that area from 200 miles west of the Mississippi to the Pacific, can testify. Out of this dissemblage Woolf makes of his work a factor of the trials of experience. Tapping the various terms of that whole sham through ironies of very immediate contact he is able to reach the explanation of "experience" and this is very beautiful to the senses because no man carries only what is under his nose.

This carries the work much beyond the personalities of movement that, say, Jack Kerouac very much comes up against. As innocent, and believable, and accurate, as that can be, it only extends what was originally a personal fervor, West, from the eastern imbecilities and selfish predicaments that were culminated in a writer such as Tom Wolfe. And popularly that was what the westward movement, or expansion, was. "Personalism" made active to the third power. The man winks at his wife and says I'll send for you. Or, I met the most interesting character on the train. But the expansion is over. It ended with the Civil War. Escapees are not home seekers. The number of people who came west seeking a home must have been *very* few, a few thousand, and the deeds of their property are still filtering down, slowly. Look at the small town newspaper, recite the names. A man will linger twenty years here, and want to go home. The native westerner is the most sad man in all the world. He has nowhere to go. The West is not a home. Think of it. No one is at home here. And the man who claims he is, by whatever device, has the saddest project of all to prove it: he invariably degenerates his arguments into his excuses, a horse, a house trailer, a spread, yes it can even constitute dry air, or he gives up and says he loves it because there are still in our time not many people here, the most pitiful grasping of all. Woolf is literally here, but Kerouac is a mere pass through, and as such, that use, amounts to no *more* than highways and hitchhikers. But there is that off-balance, that exchange that goes on between the West and the East that has changed today . . .

• • •

West is the most important geographical experience for the American, it always has been. (This is true of Europe too. Russia is the last country to the West. The American's *sense* of East is very unreal, or at best vague, and has a suspicion to it.) And it will continue to be until the continent is saturated and in that sense it is obvious it is because of the sparsity of numbers and the wealth of space. The native westerner will never be saved, he will go up against that saturation without a home to go to, and finally he will disappear in the great numbers of beings that form one saturation 200 years hence. This is a crucial time. Odysseys are made by sea and if the land can come to that requirement enough, as the American West can, by land. What happens off the earth has not been settled yet, but it will be a brand new term. In any case, the desert will be the end of it here. Loneliness. It is a very provocative state. Never fall in love with it. It is the call of death, irresistible, a practice for all the aftertime we know nothing of. And to stay away from friends now will turn out to have been the peculiar discipline of our age. That sounds ultimate. That also has not been settled; but the two or three generations at work here now are aware of it, and we separate hurrying here and there. All homes have become questionable, a man holds as many strings as possible.

● ● ●

Richard Twombly, the hero of *Fade Out,* worked in a Baltimore bank until he retired and then went to live with his daughter, in New York, an utterly terrified and watchful wife of an insurance salesman. Mr. Twombly, in the process of simply trying to live out the remainder of his days, comes up against so many of the restrictions of normal family life that he comes again to share in the state of the child: the schematism of that restriction being made bizarre by the fact that his granddaughter is set to watch over him and report on him. He is 74 years old. He has a friend of presumably the same age, and thus is set up two children but rendered in the quite believable terms of dignified old age. For instance, Mr. Twombly's interest in little girls is taken as perverse, rather than the very natural thing it is for a man of his age, having gotten quite enough of "adults" over that tenure, his former life.

Ed Behemoth, the friend, lives in like circumstance, with his daughter, whose husband is a salesman. Behemoth was once a prize fighter. He is an extraordinarily large man, one of those men the boxing profession once made use of for exhibitionary purposes. The newspapers called him a hippopotamus, and there is a definite poignancy when Behemoth, visiting the zoo with Twombly, says as of the rhinoceros, "I don't look like that," thus disclosing both his concern for his physical state and his ignorance, ignorance here being passable for innocence. When Behemoth sees the hippo emerge from the muddy tank, he is silent.

Behemoth is addicted to TV. (By the way, *Fade Out* is an expert guide to what TV *is*.) As a device to get him out of the house, Behemoth is encouraged to sell Christmas cards and so the two take off on that project together. It is one of the spots that Woolf makes commentary on "selling" but at the same time imbues with a deep poignancy: when Behemoth discovers his brother-in-law has given him Valentine cards which are even further off the mark (they thought they were trying to peddle Christmas cards in September); all he can say is, "Shit, Dick," and there are the beginnings of tears in his eyes. These are men who are over 70.

Every page has an adventure. It is not the point to go into them. It is a very exciting story, very exciting, and touching, but full of the cruelty of seemingly casual life. You hold your breath in the reading. The point is that they escape to the West. And on the trip they meet denizens. The story has a lovely ending, a very hard thing to bring off in our day.

• • •

Woolf is full of triumphs of that sort. In *Wall to Wall* he is attempting the trip back again. You remember we started in L.A. with *The Hypocritic Days*. We start there again. The novels seem serial to me, but that might be unfairly anticipating the author. *Fade Out* is a tour de force. I.e., in the focus of that quest he made the case for a sort of man no one of us has gotten to be yet. The variation of types is the easiest task a writer has, they are sitting ducks as it were, but to cross the lines of time, age, is a different matter.

Wall to Wall begins with Claude Squires, a young man not quite as young as Charles Ashton. He works (by now he works) in an insane asylum. (Incidently, I don't think Woolf can so easily be identified with his leading characters and in that sense he is off key again, in present modes. Rather, it seems, he plays composite tunes thus reaching all men like a magic harp; also, it gives his leading characters a sharp bitterness of their own, rather than what has become the habit of modern prose, to make those transfers easily to one's "self." In other words, Woolf is not "familiar" at all, and so he is very accurate in his currency: some men are difficult, all men are important, but distinctions are manifest: thus his statement— "literature, like all communication should help us to know one another, meet our friends and our enemies.")

What this leads to is simple enough: when Jack Kerouac is running back and forth across the country on wild trips, goose chases, he's fine, and one loves to go along, I do, anyway, there is nothing pleases me more than an interesting trip. But when he tries to tell me, as in *Dharma Bums,* that one of the major American problems is TV, I just want to say oh fuckit, come on. Let's start the motor up again. Now some writers can make those sociologies clear. Woolf can. But he never, never rants in that way. He never lets cant into his show. He very rightly knows, as of method as well as reality, that these machines cannot be dissuaded. They can be shown. And their showing is at least as interesting as TV itself. Take this example of cops:

> Claude looked back at the road, saw that there were two cars parked there now. The one in the rear also had tall antennas, and a cop was out and walking around the beast carefully. His white uniform, sunburned and sand-

blasted, needed laundering. Now he interrupted his tour to
look out at the desert. Claude looked around too, but he
was alone there, he and the saguaros. He walked back to
the road, hands at sides, clearly visible, bearing humility.
No man in his right mind approaches a cop without such
an offering.

"Are you the owner of this car?" A cop has something
you don't have, something you gave him earlier.

"No, I'm just delivering it to Oklahoma City for a
lady."

"Do you have plates for this car?" A cop needn't be
vicious, but he can be so, safely.

"Do you have the registration?" Presidents and pre-
miers can annihilate millions, but only a cop can explain
away your solitary murder.

"Well, I have this card here."

The officer took the card carefully with his left hand,
then lowered his eyes to it. He can be far psycho—and lock
you up, forevermore. "Are you Claude Squires?"

"Yes I am."

"Is this your signature here?"

"No, that's my father's. He owns the A-1 Drive-Away
Agency, and I'm delivering this car to Mrs. Merritt in Oklahoma City for him."

"How did he get possession of this car?"

"I don't know. I suppose Mrs. Merritt left it with him."

"Who's this Mrs. Merritt?"

Shrugging Claude said, "I never saw her."

The officer continued his tour of the car. He pried at
the hood with his fingers, and Claude reached through the
window to release it for him. After raising the hood, the
officer went back to his own car for a flashlight, returning
selected a sharp rock from the roadbed. Now he leaned
over the fender to scrape slime from the motor, compared

the number there with the one on the card. For the minute or two the cop remained there folded, up on tiptoe, with rock and flashlight clanking inside, Claude felt his own life hang in the cop's tense awkward balance. Any but the most discreet, toward gesture, any unplanned move or sound, a sneeze, itch, a gnat in the ear, would have been enough to finish him. He even knew the precise spot in his belly where he would be blasted; it shivered. Claude made no move to soothe it. Pivoting slowly the perfect murderer said, "Those numbers don't coincide."

Some writing is already way ahead of the game insofar as it is spun out of the content of the given writers who wander about. Thus the social sciences linger on the periphery of the best prose waiting for the final returns. This is a simple enough consequence. The one difference a writer has is that he may be anywhere within certain limits, at any given time. The "studies" of course are up to men who cannot move, and who, if they could, would be quite embarrassed to. What John Stuart Mill had to say about Freedom is still less interesting than the movements of Jude over one little shire.

• • •

Wall to Wall is a cleavage of the western term: it runs to the East only as a turning place for its energy. *Fade Out* has some mood in it, you don't handle old men without that— Nestor is still that kind of brooding, whether one knows it or not, the atrophied, inside mind, goes back to him. The Hebraic examples are too loaded with an exhausted religiosity. Introvert is truly what Twombly is. The introvert is polite. That's Greek, and we come back into that reality not by any cultural term but by a happy, however stupid, surplus. Codes. *Fade Out* is a code. It ought to replace the Gideon Bible in hotel rooms where old men might see it. America has been silly long enough, given the step up of time. Now, it would seem true, 200 years is enough, then you ought to get off the pot. Woolf's prose is good and very up to date because it goes toward the first beginning of a code inside the prose of these boundaries. Olson has been doing this for 15 years, but poetry heightens the voice, not the written word of man.

Wall to Wall is a true odyssey because it is an uneven line and it divorces itself from the man in question to the extent it is a story. You can't have an odyssey if you leave the single man to any real extent. The greatness of the tale will exist in the happenings as knots, along the line of his travels. Woolf uses the presence of persons with great adaptability. "He" is for you to instantly recognize behind the billboard. "I" is beside the point: it could be anyone. "She" is Vivien, an old love. Pete is looking in the window, and his dream is to claim his kingship in Mexico (the same as the gas station) which is a spread only of possibility, and something that, to those who have figured out such things, ought to have died, as a desire, long ago. Good. It still lives in the form of what people take to be their inheritance. Think still ought to be. Abstract good? Something we come to by way of a spurious training. We stay smug and still in our houses with it. It is the shades of our lamps.

There are certain constituents that are important to Woolf. Dogs are coyotes. That's more brooding. There aren't many left, but some. There are *no* wolves. They have all gone to the northern timber, the barrens of Canada. He is very compelled by abandoned towns. Popularly known as ghost towns, the bonanza trail. There is a very articulated love scene in an abandoned town (Perhaps), in *Wall to Wall*. In other places, for Woolf's purposes the abandoned town is a Promised Land.

There are few great love scenes in American literature. The abandoned town seems an ultimate sort of proposition. It certainly is peculiarly western now. The *search* took a long time but the working was of short order. I think Woolf is tapping on a fundamental reality and extracting the truth. (He makes a distinction between truth and reality.) Everything in the West gets exhausted, very quickly. From Chittenden's furs to the present uranium. The cop frankly is trying to protect something that is already a long way toward exhaustion? mines? No. Of course not. In the East the cop is a real nuisance because the social terms for such happiness as those people could have, have already been worked out, and then refused. But here in the West the cop is just such a local manifestation as Woolf makes him in the passage quoted. In the East, one might conceivably ask of a cop the direction. In the West? Never! And there you get to an essential difference. In the West, having got there, if you don't know where you're going, you would be stupid and green horn indeed if you asked other than the most sympathetic looking, the most corresponding looking man you met. But it is easier on the other hand in this spareness, to tell. I can go down anytime I want to and know, on the streets, who are my friends. Just by the look. The way they are carrying themselves, the way they dress. There are very few people in the West, but they show. Sparsity. Here is another sign. A man told me not long ago that Madrid, New Mexico, an abandoned mining town with many empty houses in it, had been taken by the AEC and intentionally contaminated for tests. Don't try to go. An open ear is the most valuable instrument a man can have out here.

[Pocatello, 1963]

A Cup of Coffee

to the memory of M.L.

A society or country that loses interest in revolution and comes to fear that state of affairs is very dull. The U.S., Canada, South Africa and such countries, socially and politically are dull. Very dull. Mexico is an interesting country and a generation ago must have been more. Violence, when the terms are social and political, and not clinical (world power), is not necessarily beside the point. Civil rights is a proposition. The whole people is asked to lie down flat on its back and take it in the belly. The well-to-do in any case, in any country, in any race, and in any class of that race, have always been able to get along without concerning themselves with that proposition. In the U.S. the question is sinister not because there are broad swaths of people who need a fair shake, but because there is no part of the proposition that will ever recognize or, more to the point, allow those in need, or even simply on the street, to be that, there. Curfew. Time is a location. More property.

There is a tax on any man's time. Economic. Rulers always boost the Time of their subjects. But you are supposed to think it something else. The newest weapons, like the oldest, work only on men.

Sounds vague. But no vaguer than any example. A man I know downtown in a filling station told me of an incident this past spring. Two Mexicans came into Pocatello to work in the sugar beets or was it potatoes. They arrived. It was several miles out to the farm which was on reservation land. (Some whites have extensive farms within the Indian land. Figure that out.) The farmer could not be contacted at that hour, or would not come into town for them so the workers were faced with spending the night in town. Finally, and because it is dangerous to try staying on the streets, they were advised to go to the Salvation Army. The Army gave them passes or coupons of some kind to get a hotel room. They tried several hotels and were refused. It would have been the same if they had had cash. So this filling station attendant let them sleep on some tires in back of the grease rack. They appreciated it. He appreciated their smiles. The local drunk tank is used for lots of people. You don't have to be drunk to get there. A notorious place. Lots of men over the past few years, but mostly Mexicans and Indians, have had their heads caved in completely by the unstoppable boots of deputies and cops. No one at all in the U.S. imagines that, if drunk and obnoxious and on his way Home, a lawyer would be in serious danger. Murder, even, perhaps especially in his case would be easily explained away. Of course there is once in a while a doctor who gets hung up with a mistress and the law but it seems accidental and is certainly sensational. So what.

Negroes, Mexicans, Indians, Whites don't seem awfully special. It is just that, black brown white, divisions, not complex, subject to broad and crude considerations only. A goddamn cup of stinking coffee at Walgreens. Pew! I am ashamed that my brothers get stopped because of their color or the way they dress. It seems simply correct that Mississippi and Alabama and South Africa be occupied. If it were my decision, those places and a few others would be occupied tomorrow. Talk *is* cheap. Talk about "human rights" is particularly cheap. Rights have nothing to do with general colors, shapes of eyes or forms of noses. Never. Anyone might be in danger, or might be safe, but that will be determined by the incredible meanness with which America handles its people, always has handled them. The ethic is behavioral. I am a poet. It seems to me a point of honor and deep responsibility that I not number among my friends a cop, or a doctor or lawyer, or a President of the United States, or the head of an insane asylum, or a gangster. Or anyone who thinks Negroes should stay in their place and be lynched. In the meantime, how I take any given man will be my own affair, always subject to more critical factors, how he carries his body, the cast of his eyes, the tone and cadence of his voice. Race *is* an exotic recognition, mostly visual, and always a momentary interest.

[Pocatello, 1963]

Two Non-Reviews

I. LEROI JONES' *DUTCHMAN & THE SLAVE*

The first of these two plays was produced at the Cherry Lane
Theatre in New York and won the ninth annual Obie Award
for the best American play done Off-Broadway in the 1963-
64 season. It was very much reviewed in *Time, Newsweek,
New York Times, Herald-Tribune,* etc., and as I remember the
reviews they were generally approving, they were generally
patriotic that an American Negro had come along finally and
said it hot, and direct, had been "angry" (anger is always a relief, i.e., everybody can pick up their teacups again) and had
included the White world in some active way. And that indeed
is something to be appreciative of, thankful for. There was
also the calculated degree of critical reservation, of caution.
Perhaps Mr. Jones is being a mite *un*fair. Philip Roth, the nov-
elist, I seem to remember, wanted to make the point that the
white world wasn't, or isn't, all bad. That in Real Life, the
thing probably wouldn't go that way, or at least, there would

be more Understanding, somewhere. Of course he didn't make that point, and in some more advanced culture it would have been vulgar to try. I think he finally found *Dutchman* wanting in Art, the final refuge and excuse of a sneaky thinker.

I want to speak of the history of that play in that manner and not review it here because it has been seen and reviewed a great deal. When I saw the play it charged me with the accuracy of its intelligence and emotion. It was played well. But it reads like an achievement of writing in the sense that O'Neill's Emperor's words are right, as Gover's Kitten's aren't quite. Even so, an ear that can deliver the hip-educated speech of downtown New York has to be married to an occasion of some local necessity and to a past of such common weight that it is an accumulation rather than a generation. In other words, local is simply the place, and time, what they're talking about, accumulation, is what they put into it. It could be racial. But that's just funny. Everybody, "down deep in their hearts," knows that's not true. Back of that is the rather scary notion that one's daughter might be delighted to be married to a Negro, or someone else, a Chinese man, perhaps a Finlander. No, it comes down that *any* intensity of talk is liable to put the talkers anywhere. Jones does put them there . . . "In the flying underbelly of the city. Steaming hot, and summer on top, outside. Underground. The subway heaped in modern myth." White woman, Black boy.

LULA. Weren't you staring at me through the window? At the last stop?

CLAY. Staring at you? What do you mean?

LULA. Don't you know what staring means?

CLAY. I saw you through the window . . . if that's what it means. I don't know if I was staring. Seems to me you

71

were staring through the window at me.

LULA. I was. But only after I'd turned around and saw you staring through that window down in the vicinity of my ass and legs.

CLAY. Really?

LULA. Really. I guess you were just taking those idle potshots. Nothing else to do. Run your mind over people's flesh.

CLAY. Oh boy. Wow, now I admit I was looking in your direction. But the rest of that weight is yours.

2

Between LeRoi Jones and Richard Wright stands a monument named Chester Himes. At the end, in the Fate chapter of *Native Son*, Bigger says, "I don't want to kill! But what I killed for, I *am*!" And Boris Max, who tried to steer Bigger toward a death filled with as much light as possible, lifted his hand to touch Bigger but could not, his amazement was so great as he received part of the light of that revelation. In the novels of Chester Himes, for instance *The Lonely Crusade,* 1947, and *The Third Generation,* 1954, I read an extension of what a particular black man is, or particular black men are, past Bigger, and out of the cry. Carried to the world in which that quite tortured necessity is articulate. The Native Son is a Mississippi boy and all that that means, a sort of upside down Mediterranean for those men. A post slavery man is liable to be killed but that's the least of it, the problem is how to live a life right now without *having* to kill in return, a possible act, proven, but one that will define you at the intersection of an absolute disadvantage. Inside the lines of that Alternate nation, with the ground three hundred years of living suffocation, Himes moves his men. In every paragraph of *The Third*

Generation his figure falls down an elevator shaft only to be picked up and put back so it can happen again. If you are that man, and you are not a scientific american, you might as well forget it. By the time it comes to a matter of "defense" it's probably already too late.

Jones is willing to let his men make war. War of their own determination, that's the important thing, a war of initiative instead of the hopeless, no matter how "noble" or " nonresistant," defense. Martin Luther King had better reason to have been in a position to turn down the Nobel Prize than Sartre. And it is Men. Of the Negro, it is the men who are in danger. It is their prolonged crisis, decade after decade. All women have always been acceptable. And it is the man who must have the last word, that's all he's got. The woman has another edge. The slave is argumentative. The war is raging outside town, the outskirts are being occupied. Walker is the black man, he wants that last word, because people are going to die whether their agencies for death function or not. It is more a guaranteed fact than a mystery, in the social term. Grace is Walker's former wife, remarried to a white man, Easley, Walker's old friend. She says to him,

Walker, you were preaching the murder of all white people. Walker, I was, am, white. What do you think was going through my mind every time you were at some rally or meeting whose sole purpose was to bring about the destruction of white people?

WALKER. O, goddamn it, Grace, are you so stupid? You were my wife . . . I loved you. You mean because I loved you and was married to you . . . had had children by you, I wasn't supposed to say the things I felt. I was crying out against three hundred years of oppression; not against individuals.

EASLEY. But it's individuals who are dying.

WALKER. It was individuals who were doing the oppressing. It was individuals who were being oppressed. The horror is that oppression is not a concept that can be specifically transferable. From the oppressed, down on the oppressor. To keep the horror where it belongs . . . on those people who can speak of, even in this last part of the twentieth century, as evil.

EASLEY. You're so wrong about everything. So terribly sickeningly wrong. What can you change? What do you hope to change? Do you think Negroes are better people than whites . . . that they can govern a society *better* than whites? That they'll be more judicious or more tolerant? Do you think they'll make fewer mistakes? I mean really, if the Western white man has proved one thing . . . it's the futility of modern society. So the have-not peoples become the haves. Even so, will that change the essential functions of the world? Will there be more love or beauty in the world . . . more knowledge . . . because of it?

WALKER. Probably. Probably there will be more . . . if more people have a chance to understand what it is. But that's not even the point. It comes down to baser human endeavor than any social-political thinking. What does it matter if there's more love or beauty? Who the fuck cares? Is that what the Western ofay thought while he was ruling . . . that his rule somehow brought more love and beauty into the world? Oh, he might have thought that concomitantly, while sipping a gin rickey and scratching his ass . . . but that was not ever the point. Not even on the Crusades. The point is that you had your chance, darling, now these other folks have theirs.
    (Quietly)
Now they have theirs.

EASLEY. God, what an ugly idea.

It sure is. Alarming too. And "shocking," a word often used
in connection with Jones' work. But only alarming or shocking in the same old way, which is if you got something you
like and somebody *takes* it you can be excused for getting excited. And that *is* one of the oldest habits of western civilization, taking. It is so very simple-minded it is enough to make
one laugh out loud. There are homely sayings to cover it, "the
shoe is on the other foot now," "kettle calling the pot blackie,"
and it would seem at least that any attempt to thicken the
proposition in order that we may "reason together" is to
make the pitch all over again, namely: will you please wait
here till I get back?

So all three of them have it out in that house Walker got
to past the lines, "in a large living room, tastefully furnished
the way an intelligent university professor and his wife would
furnish it." It is that crucial talk that is so important to our
kind of lives and it just has to sound important, and indispen-
sable, and phony. It's the only stuff there is to work with. The
Western World hasn't yet come on to a language it can use to
say something important, or, even, pertinent. It all has that
incredible ring of D.H. Lawrence making his characters figure
out how to conduct their sex lives. But in *The Slave* there is
the virtue of a mistaken notion to give the messages a double
take—Grace and Easley think Walker has come to kidnap his
own children. Race? That's a hard word. Sometimes our pos-
sessions suffer from a qualification we would have sworn was
not our own.

I will end this with the first part of the prologue to *The
Slave,* spoken by Walker, ". . . dressed as an old field slave,
balding, with white hair, and an old ragged vest. (Perhaps he
was sitting, sleeping, initially-nodding and is awakened by
faint cries, like a child's.) He comes to the center of the stage
slowly, and very deliberately, puffing on a pipe, and seemingly

uncertain of the reaction any audience will give his speech":

> Whatever the core of our lives. Whatever the deceit. We live
> where we are, and seek nothing but ourselves. We are liars,
> and we are murderers. We invent death for others. Stop
> their pulses publicly. Stone possible lovers with heavy
> worlds we think are ideas . . . and we know, even before
> these shapes are realized, that these worlds, these depths or
> heights we fly to smoothly, as in a dream, or slighter, when
> we stare dumbly into space, leaning our eyes just behind a
> last quick moving bird, then sometimes the place and twist
> of what we are will push and sting, and what the crust of
> our stance has become will ring in our ears and shatter that
> piece of our eyes that is never closed. An ignorance. A stu-
> pidity. A stupid longing not to know . . . which is automat-
> ically fulfilled. Automatically triumphs. Automatically
> makes us killers or foot-dragging celebrities at the core of
> any filth. And it is a deadly filth that passes as whatever
> thing we feel is too righteous to question, too deeply felt
> to deny.

II. LEROI JONES' *BLUES PEOPLE*

That a white american could feel a part of this book or these
people in any *easy* sense would be hard to defend. Jazz writers, or the looser types of sociologists have always had to hide
their embarrassment behind a kind of gratuitous enthusiasm.
That writing has always stank of that act. Or intention. For
the first time it is explained to me calmly that those blacks
"transported" to america were people. Through some ruse I
was lead to understand they were "negroes." Before I came to
understand that social anthropology is a false endeavor in the
sense that when you look at a certain feature you're supposed
to associate it with the catalogue of which it is a part, before
I ever knew even on casual terms a negro I was misled to

think of them as a problem that wanted a "sensible" solution. Back in my small home town, eastern Illinois, in high school there was a small group, three or four, who listened to jazz. As I remember we came in along with Don Byas. I didn't know the difference so I liked Charlie Ventura too. But we had the sense, even if part of it was a use, i.e., I know about something you've never heard of, to like Coleman Hawkins best of all. There was that glamor too that Lionel Hampton had discovered the vibraphone or xylophone in an attic somewhere and mastered it in 30 minutes. We weren't prepared to recognize any limitation there. There was that time too I liked what Leonard Feather had to say and the way he said it, also *Downbeat,* and that was when only the initiated could unfold that magazine without tearing it apart.

Blues People: Negro Music in White America is an intelligent book and that fact alone makes it more than another book on jazz. Or more than an ordinary "new interpretation." There are no devices of thought, happily. Mr. Jones is certainly intelligent, not that that's such a great virtue (think of the "intelligent" men good men everywhere have been subject to, much to the latter's horror): the attractive thing is that he's an astonishing and clear writer. If anyone doubts such usefulness let him go through the great dead jargonesque material called the history of jazz, to name only one area this book describes. No one told me *banjo* was an african word. I never had the wit to ask, true, but volunteered information is nice. The idea that the early african american pined to go home touches me more than I could have guessed. It is an important thing to think about, the effects of such yearning, more certainly than the great grey state called slavery wherin nothing much is distinguished, least of all that the nature of their familiar west african slave practice was quite different from the new american captivity. And that they registered their preoccupation with going back home using a foreign religion whose terms of place are notably abstract; *they* knew the *whereabouts* of the river Jordan. That Blues are more a poetry of speech than a music is an idea of great appeal. That I can otherwise read in a record liner that the Blues has a cesura likeable to that of Pope's is an idea of insupportably pretentious vulgarity.

I can see no mistakes in this book. If the author maintains his present clarity of mind I would guess his future to be ambiguous, and by that I mean he might be encouraging the vicissitudes to a greater degree than the terms of ordinary success call for. Happen what may, the spirit of this book and of its author cannot fail.

[Pocatello, 1964]

The Outcasts
of Foker Plat
NEWS FROM THE STATES

Di nova pena mi conven far versi
   e dar matera al ventesimo canto
   della prima canzon, ch'è de' sommersi,
Io era già disposto tutto quanto
   a riguardar nello scoperto fondo,
   che si bagnava d'angoscioso pianto;
e vidi gente per lo vallon tondo
   venir, tacendo e lagrimando, al passo
   che fanno le letane in questo mondo,
Come 'l viso me scese in lor più basso,
   mirabil-mente apparve esser travolto
   ciascun tra 'l mento e 'l principio del casso;
che dalle reni era tornato il volto,
   ed in dietro venir li convenià,
   perchè 'l veder dinanzi era lor tolto.

               —Canto XX, Inferno

i

    To begin with, since we are in a foreign country (and who isn't), let's take it right out of the mail:

. . . I just picked up my 1966 horoscope and it looks like
its going to be a big year for me. one thing that looks im-
pressive is that LEOS are supposed to really groove with
birds—other *leos* who are famous

> paul anka
> napoleon b
> leo durocher
> eddie fisher
> alfred hitchcock
> herbert hoover
> van johnson
> jacqueline kennedy
> robert mitchum
> peter o'toole
> robert taylor

and my holy shit thank god herman melville i thought for
a minute . . . i was grooving in the wrong field

And from the same bright metropolitan jewel on the West
Coast comes another if slightly different dispatch:

. . . I could, literally, "kill, kill, kill for peace!" And it has
changed H——, among others, and, most certainly, myself.
I have tasted power, granted, by popular consent, used it.
(It is a most valuable and amusing involvement) There have
been casualties and desertions and I think of Washington at
v.f. and that Woodward missed that, not to give anything
more to george than that it wasn't easy, even evil, even
good, not easy. not that by any stretch a shitty bloodless
power scuffle remotely connects with v.f., or, me, or
george w. or, adam clayton powell. just that the work, 8
hour day five days a week is unbelievably ugly after more
than one and ½ years . . . which, is, my own particular now
amphetamine life spurt that keeps me hopping at the green
beret level, ceasing fire only on holidays. And did have a

fine Christmas with the W****** and other friends. I cooked and J**** stuffed a fat goose and people brought other things and D*** and myself bought mucho juice—brandy for eggnog, sparkling burgundy for the food, bourbon and cognac for after dinner, and there was grass and hashish and a real american good time, lots of babies, children, pretty women, confident men, flushed cheeks, rock and roll, whatever!

ii

Ed Sanders, LeRoi Jones, Michael McClure, Robert Duncan, and John Wieners. That's a partial list, to be sure, of the men who have to be salamandrine indeed to survive on those grim shores.

Ed Sanders is John Wyclif 1380 announcing the end of transubstantiation, or the beginning, which way you choose to look at it. In an interview in "The Village Square" the interviewer asks:

What is people's first reaction to the title *Fuck You/a magazine of the arts*?
Occasionally a reader will go insane with rage. Tight-assed people sometimes giggle. Some let their eyes glaze over and look bored. At cocktail parties in Michigan they burn it. The Mexican border police register disgust. But most are friendly and very curious.
Do you ever bother to justify or explain it?
Of course. I usually try to explain what I'm doing: A word should have one basic meaning; a lovely word like fuck, or fuck you, should not have hateful, pejorative connotations. I try to explain about the LSD Communarium, freedom for hallucinogens, God through cannabis, grope for peace, etc., etc.
What is the philosophy that guides your choice of content?
The philosophy of Total Assault on the Culture. I print the

poetry I like plus occasional free-verse gutter doggerel. As for the editorials, notes on contributors, peace statements, and Egyptian freak-doodles, I pretend that the United States is a very permissive asylum, and act accordingly.

Who finances *Fuck You*?

A leading Ezra Pound scholar, a millionaire painter, an up-town publisher, and a cartel of 17 Times Square toe queens.

Is there an official price: Do you charge anybody?

I give *Fuck You/a magazine of the arts* away free, as they come out. Complete runs of all back issues I sell to university libraries and collectors to help finance new issues. Many of the major universities in the country have full sets.

Why did the FBI visit you?

They think I'm wonderful.

What are some of your other activities?

Co-editor of the *Marijuana Newsletter,* formed to promote legalization of marijuana; I operate the Peace Eye Book-store and Scrounge Lounge, in the lower East Side; I'm publisher and editor of several anthologies of poetry, a-mong them *Banana, Despair, Bugger,* and *Suck;* I'm a vet-eran East Side bar creep. Currently I'm shooting short films at my secret movie studio to show with the Fug songs. That is, I'm creating a movie/music system called the Fugitone: among the first to be shot are "Coca Cola Douche," "Bull Tongue Clit," and the "I Saw the Best Minds of My Generation Rock."*

Sanders is *the* medicine man of our era. He looks like the man who *could* have shot Lincoln but didn't. All the fabulous force of his shamanism is thrown into the "total assault on the culture." Ladies and gents in this bottle I have here all

---

*John Wilcock's column, *Los Angeles Free Press,* 8226 Sunset Boulevard, Hollywood 46, California. June 15, 1965.

culture, after just a leetle shake I'll cure the sick, libraries queue on the right and have your hundred dollars ready (coin please, no paper), everybody else help yourselves. But it's all TRUE. This is no legerdemain. The cold cream jar really did belong to Allen Ginsberg. And whereas movie stars think of themselves as movie stars, Ed Sanders *is* a movie star. A true Fug-star. The first hero we've had who could stand up to all those russian chinese examples. But the *peace* is real too. Not some sticky use of it, Averell Harriman making weird side trips to see Tito, or Humphrey bland as a condom to the Philippines to con some "dark" people into the right side of the conflict. When you see the Fugs perform you see that what's happening is important, it's a grope-group. Groping is not violent, but it isn't, equally, non-violent. Peace has become confused. Perhaps everyone has forgotten what it was. What was it? At the Berkeley Poetry Conference last summer when Charles Olson made an intricate point the cap of which was "War is Beauty," Sanders objected, "I'm a peace freak, myself." That's no special conflict. Beauty is not Sanders' stick, particularly. But culture is. Word-culture. What he says, the Ra he draws in the men's john. And culture is total. I'm thinking of that Fox-Frobenius article in the September 3, 1936 *New English Weekly.* "Culture is an independent organism. Man is not its subject, but rather its object or bearer. Man does not produce culture. Culture permeates man." Ed Sanders is not anything so simple as a "product" of the smallish and relatively insignificant insane asylum called America: the introduction to his book of poems *Peace Eye* notes: ". . . it takes the earth/ to make a feather fall." No matter how much less the Beatles are than the Fugs there is more connection between them than the Fugs and Bob Dylan. "Day Tripper" is accurate if light. And the Fugs have managed to avoid the heavy literalness of folk singers' blank verse. The Wobblies were lovely people and their ghosts inevitably travel free on the buses of the American conscience but they *are* dead. To show how happily the Fugs freak through the American scene here's a song by Sanders from the Fugs' Songbook:

COCA-COLA DOUCHE

My baby ain't got no money,
But her snatch it taste like honey
Cause she makes that
        Coca-Cola douche.

My baby she fizzes & she fuzzes,
But her pussy it snaps like a turtle
Cause she makes that
        Coca-Cola douche.

My baby she humps like a wildcat,
Her pelvis got the caffeine shakes
Cause she makes that
        Coca-Cola douche.

My baby is straight from heaven
My baby you can sip with a straw
Cause she makes that
        Coca-Cola douche.

My baby sends me out for some ice cream,
She said,
'Come on down for an ice cream soda;
I just had that
        Coca-Cola douche.'*

(There is an informative article in the December 24, 1965 issue of *Peace News* on the Fugs, Sanders and Tuli Kupferberg.)

---

*Copyright 1965 by Ed Sanders.

84

Robert Duncan in two fairly recent poems I've seen, one in *Peace News,* London, and earlier "The Multiversity" in *Synapse,* Berkeley, has made evident the stretch of his attendance. The angle of his practice is wide indeed. From the overwhelmingly beautiful "Lammas Dream Poem" in *Paris Review* 36, with the powerful recurrence "my mother would be a falconress" through its medieval veins to the multiversity, Kerr and Strong, no dream at all, the real hydras:

> not men   but heads of the hydra
>
>> his false faces in which
>> authority lies
>
>> hired minds of private interests
>
>>> over us
>
> here: Kerr (behind him heads of the Bank of America,
>>> the Tribune,
>>>> heads of usury, heads of war)
>
>>> the worm's   mouthpiece   spreds
>
>>>> what it wishes   its own
>
> false news : 1) that the students broke into Sproul's office, vandalizing, creating disorder; 2) that the Free Speech Movement has no wide support, only an irresponsible minority   going on strike

And the poem ends:

>> Each day   the last day;   each day   the
>
>>> beginning   the first word
>
>>>> door of the day or law awakening we create,
>
>>> vowels sung in a field in mid-morning

Evil "referred to the root of *up, over*"
    simulacra of law that wld over-rule
      the Law man's inner nature seeks,
  coils about them,   not men but

    heads and armors of the worm   office is

    There being no common good, no commune
    no communion, outside the freedom of

      individual volition.

"A conspiracy for freedom." Just that. Nothing fancy, Only what the words mean, What evil *means.* A lot of people seem to think affairs at Berkeley are unusual or unique. "Town and gown used daggers, swords, and even bows and arrows in their pitched battles in High Street. In 1355 the townsmen made a regular massacre of clerks and students; the survivors fled in terror from Oxford, and the University closed down until the King intervened to protect and avenge the scholars. At Cambridge, in the riots of 1381, the town destroyed the University charters and records.

"The medieval student, before the development of the college system had done its work, was riotous, lawless, and licentious. He was miserably poor; he often learnt very little for want of books and tutoring, and left without taking a degree. Yet many were enthusiastically eager for learning or at least for controversy. Some were only fourteen years old, but most were of an age rather more nearly resembling that of modern undergraduates."* This clash was between academicians who defended the liberties of their university against papal interference. What, in our day, is the Pentagon if not Papacy. It *is* also the Church. Everyone must have noticed or

---

*J.M. Trevelyan, *Illustrated English Social History.* (Pelican Books, 1964), Vol.I, p.116.

TV what a fine pair the Pope and Johnson made.

iv

    In another ecclesiastical area the poet and playwright Le-
Roi Jones has shifted into the most absolutist position of all.
With his early plays, *Dutchman, The Slave, The Toilet,* he out-
lined what I think must have been for him the prolegomena
to a transfer back into a world he was of but had not been
wholly part of. Harlem is not his native ground. When Malcolm X was assassinated there was clearly no other intellectual leadership equal to Jones in those ranks. Malcolm had just
begun to make headway through the terrible delicate discriminations between the mass masochism of Martin Luther King,
whose political pyramid includes at the base some less Christian but still willing student movements, and the sectarian
secretary-pinching paternalism of Elijah Muhammed. LeRoi
Jones has been unable to assure that leadership for various and
complex reasons. The Negro people do not have just one
white enemy in America. There are hundreds of different
kinds of white men all in their phantasmagoric masks—and
not just white men—Red men, Brown men, Yellow men,
Green men. That's right. Green men hate black men too. But
white is the medium of it all. Just as the American Indian refers to certain acculturated Indians, though they be "full-
bloods" as *white Indians,* there are white Negroes, and not
the ones Norman Mailer, because he fancies marijuana, had in
mind. Anyone can put on a white collar, and isn't collar a funny word.
    The absoluteness of LeRoi Jones' position is correct. He
says, "THE WHITE MAN IS OBSOLETE." which sounds right. He
also says, "most American white men are trained to be fags."
Which sounds pretty provocative—I always wonder what
those astronauts do for fourteen days up there in "space."
See the January, 1966 issue of *Cavalier.*

V

The work of Michael McClure (*Dark Brown, The New Book/A Book of Torture,* etc.) could be taken as some poetic form of zoanthropy by the superficial reader. The verse form, the vertical urge of his lines could seem unbounded if one did not grasp that his whole attention has been directed *in* with such concentration that the rush goes right out again into the limbs—to the tingling points where contact, if it is ever made, is made with all the biological circuits plugged in. Early in 1965 a printed booklet appeared from him with the cancelled portrait of Billy the Kid on the cover. *Poisoned Wheat* is the title. It begins:

OH, BLUE GRAY GREEN PALE GRAHHR!
TRANQUIL POURING ROSE LION SALT!

There is death in Viet Nam!
There is death in Viet Nam!
There is death in Viet Nam!
And our bodies are mad with the forgotten
memory that we are creatures!

Blue-black skull rose lust boot!

Citizens of the United States
are in the hands of traitors
who ignore their will and force
them into silent acceptance
of needless and undesired warfare.

EACH MAN, WOMAN, CHILD

is innocent
and not responsible
for the atrocities committed by any
government. Mistakes, hypocrisies, crimes

that result in the present
FASCISM
are made in the past in
HISTORY.
Structural mechanisms of Society
create guilt in the individual.

He says:

I AM NOT GUILTY!

I AM A LIVING CREATURE!

I AM NOT RESPONSIBLE FOR THE TRAITOROUS
FASCISM AND TOTALITARIANISM
THAT SURROUND me!!!

and

CAPITALISM IS FAILURE!
It creates overpopulation, slavery,
and starvation.

Whether I be in Soviet Russia, Red China, or Imperialist
England or France, or Capitalist United States
I am not responsible for the fascist
or totalitarian crimes
that are whitewashed
under the title *Modern History!*

it ends:

THE UNIVERSE IS MESSIAH!

WHAT IS THIS SMOKE?

The neon napalm flash is filth and death!

GRAHH!   BLESS!

"Watchman what of the night" is a short prose-poem
John Wieners wrote about his withdrawal from the early
morning amphetamine alleys and streets of San Francisco,
New York and Boston. I heard it on the tape of his reading at
the Berkeley Poetry Conference. It is a strange statement. An
intelligent man hearing it said to me, "but the poems are so
much clearer on that reality, this just seems a negation of all
his poems." But I don't know. The poems are beautiful indeed—*The Hotel Wentley Poems* is probably the most famous
testament in American poetry of the outlands of the modern
city, of the ikons in the crumbled mansions of a half-lit drug
world. And *Ace of Pentacles,* 1964, set up what seem the
forms of a new mythology of the streets, inner rooms, the
veiled windows, signs no social study will ever discover because the poet alone has been there and insists, a little unrea-
sonably some would say, on casting it all into poems:

> And I am lost beside the furs
> and homburgs at Fifth and
> Fifty Seventh where Black Starr
> And Frost holds
>
> its annual sale of diamonds.
> Precious stones aloft
> in the zones of heaven.
> Haven of the heart,
>
> This is the new start, that
> long at last awaited journey
> to the stars, who stay
> at the Chatham, Gotham and Pierre.

"You talk of going but don't even have a suitcase." Or
anything to put in it. "You sit a naked cool rider/ and now
watch the windows open by themselves." "and I have known/

despair that the Face has ceased to stare/ at me with the Rose of the world/ but lies furled." "I will materialize in Paradise one day soon . . ." And he may have done it:

CHINOISERIE

Birds of paradise float in green lagoons,

while painted canopies stretch over
    Chinese couples

sunning themselves in gowns of feathered
    silk.

Palms from the Orient flower on banks
    of miniature islands

garnered in reeds and peony blossoms,
    bloomers

of white grace the flanks of a Javanese
    saint.

Boats are propelled by poles of bamboo,

held in the hands of dreamers; the holds
    are heavy

with fruit and dates; and they paddle
    through clouds

of azure drifting in canals of heaven.

vii

Where does it all go? In one way it depresses me that the articulation of beauties and the playing of the vectors of pain against the night sky like a search light probing for bombers, seem to go on in a solution of only salt—the negatives breed at an alarming rate. For instance, I'm not at all sure Robert Duncan should use even a little of his immense energies on creatures such as Clark Kerr or Chancellor Strong. I'm afraid they are nothing so wonderful as dragons to be slain. And I don't mean by that it's a *waste of time*—Poetry is an organ of the tongue, it makes it own time. But any "protest" might become a crashing bore . . . like Berkeley that "great University" is a crashing bore. (A young man of Cambridge University asked me in all seriousness if a political poem could be valid. Plainly he thought it couldn't. One wonders who his tutors are.) Sanders is another man of course. He's young and maybe somebody does use coca-cola to douche with. Some far-out types *must* have taken that hint. Sounds fine. Where it will end I've tried before to think and never can. That LeRoi Jones, a mesaba of intelligence, is an exile in his own country is interesting: a country which prides itself on its resources and vehemently forgets the fantastic shadowed face of Exploitation stares from the window of the rear coach, clickety-clack, all the way back. Everybody out! Man those tanks in Watts, cordon off those streets! And McClure is standing there in the dim light of the burning buildings in his beast suit—"Slit my throat over my bowl. White bowl. The red/ dripping OH. OHHHHHHHHHHHHH. No wit not even/ Shit fakery shit. OhhhhhHHHH!"

[Colchester, 1965]

92

The Poet,
the People, the Spirit

INTRODUCTION

The contents of this speech and *The Shoshoneans,* the book
it anticipates, were both the product of the summer of 1965,
rather ahead of what was to become, and to a certain extent
continues to be, a fashionable concern for the social and cultural appurtenances of native american life. The politican and
economic actualities of course remain enshrouded in the un-
altered patterns of avarice which stretch from the chambers
of commerce local to the chambers of the federal bureau of
investigation. Transactions were clearer, over the fiercer part
of native-white history, when affairs were subsumed under
the Department of War. The bureau of indian affairs is one
of the early linguistic deceptions in a trend which has now
become pervasive, and which is the medium of a raging disease of the national outlook. One is bombarded by the flak
of indignation over cruelty to animals but not even a phrase
of time for the starveling Sioux. It is the function of the

"social worker" to rob "the case." Our shock at the public examples is meant to absorb the otherwise unincorporable bitterness of our knowledge.

The nature of the expression about to come under view, and to a certain extent its occasion, is marked by a variety of peculiarities, I noticed as I reread it. In the first place, its awkwardness is extreme even for something which was not originally a verbally ordered text. The problem is not that I do not do this kind of thing well, but that the material was at that time merely accumulated, and in any event there never was the configuration of a conventional story. Rather, the matter was, although at times linear, disconnected from reservation to reservation and from individual to individual. And, in fact, apparently, that could serve as a general description of how it is with the people of the basin plateau too.

From our experience we know this predicament to be not universal. The situation in the newest theatre of conflict, Alaska, is otherwise in many significant ways. Subsistence there has been marked by the richness of the marine life on the continental shelf and by the existence of a vast reservoir of large mammalia with all their by-products. There was famine at times, and disease, both alcoholic and viral, was certainly introduced. Nevertheless, labor and wit could always have application. And although dangerous, the northern winter, which season is much of the year, provided a stability of travel which was unknown in the basin. Dogs can't get much to pull across alkali and sand.

In both these instances one can see how the terms of prior existence come forward into the present. In Alaska the people, who were always enthusiastic and able traders, now fly as well as float and slide, the first and last modes very often over their own continuous ground. Now they appear to be in good shape as the latest and biggest invasion of honkers finally clomp in to save the environment. This is to speak in

such wide and soft contrast as the Advantaged and the Dis-
advantaged, but the effect, which we call "recreation" is common to both locations, whether that be mountain climbing,
moose killing, or crap shooting.

Another, and quite secondary peculiarity, was the circumstance in which I was "invited" to give this talk. I was not
actually asked to attend the Berkeley Conference of the summer of 1965, but went as a substitute forced on the organiz-
ers of the conference by LeRoi Jones, who had begun to with-
draw from such contact. And that's how I went along as the
indian.

As a further note, it is my pleasure to thank Bob Rose
and Derryll White for transcribing the raw tape, cutting it
back, restringing it, and thereby generally enhancing its sense.

Jimtown, 30 Sept. '76

[Drops something on the floor, laughter.] That might be luc-
ky. Gee, I had a slip of paper. The title of the lecture, "The
Poet, The People, The Spirit" was sort of quick. And I didn't
really have anything in mind: I assure you, it has no meaning.
It simply was a kind of inclusiveness that I knew I could talk
inside of, in the sense that I must at this point know something about all those things. At the time I decided to come
down here I had just come back from Nevada *with* Leroy Mc-
Lucas, taking pictures of Indians, he was. I was tagging along
making notes, looking. I was really looking at the kind of terrible awesomeness of the miscellania of American upper landscape, what's superficially on it, the geography. What's resting
on top of it.

[Draws on blackboard.] Here's Nevada and Idaho, Wyoming, Utah. The Paiutes, the Northern Paiutes and the Northern Shoshonis stretching from Fort Washington in Wind
River to Reno, are laying claim to a land mass that's like this,

approximately. That's a lot of territory to claim. What they're
after is, not the land back, which is obviously impossible. All
those white people are not going to move off easily once
they've established farms and bought tractors, built dams. So
what the Indians want is *money* payment for it, in some way.
Well, it's hard to say what money is. It's very difficult to say
what money is. It's difficult to say what money is to an Indian. Very often you—it's awfully hard to talk to Indians by the
way, because they don't speak English, except, you know, in
the most casual sense. And you don't speak Shoshoni, at all.
So they want a dollar for their picture. Something like that.
Well that's not much. Leroy McLucas of course, is used to
being asked much more than that. So he thought they were
pretty square in that sense. But they say "a dollar," you know,
"I want a dollar." All right well here's a dollar, everybody's
got a dollar. And it doesn't mean anything, except that occasionally you'll come across the Indian who is really depressed
and wants fifty cents. And then that *really* makes you open
your eyes and wonder about *that* person. What relationship
does he have to this nation? What sense does he have of it?
Where does he think he is? What does he think of us? Quite
obviously such a strange pair as myself and Leroy McLucas,
who is a Negro, approaching American Indians with the idea
of photographing them is . . . well might be a loaded proposition in every, every step of the way. And it was. So you
don't go up and say "How!", although that might amuse them
too because they're not humorless people. But you have to
somehow get out to someplace where you're just a man,
there. And you . . . have to make them know that. Well they
don't know that though. Because you are a man. And that's
the precise thing they fear. They don't frankly trust American Negroes or even like them very much. And not at all on
. . . it's not racial in any sense that I could feel. But very
much cultural. Very much that . . . the American Negro is pre-

cisely wrong because he wants to enter the mainstream American life. That's *the* reason he's wrong. Racially, he's just another man to an Indian. And that was a relief along those . . . Route 40 for instance, where you get so much of the southern element all over the West. The red neck, the red of which has faded a little bit, but all of the kind of incipient hostility is there. Perhaps even more viciously because it is, you know, about to spring out, and not on the surface. We all know that, as many Negroes do *know,* that it's easier to meet the hostility directly than in some unpredictable way.

Okay. So there you are, right there with the first, with the natives, with the first people, the first human beings . . . on this continent. And you don't know what to say to them. You can't say, "Well look I'm a poet and if . . . so that means that even if I'm not, even a good poet, I don't have to be a good poet actually. But if I'm a true poet . . . you can trust me to be sympathetic. You can trust me to know that you're Indian and that this man is a Negro. And we're not here to really . . . shame you or take *bad* pictures or *anything* like that." You know. But I mean you can't say that. They wouldn't understand that at all. Not at all. And I can see and I can understand their not understanding it. It seems to me that the national life creates a situation in which any person who goes out to do something is thwarted by the fact that he is stigmatized already if he comes from this nation. Right inside the nation. I'm not talking about the "Ugly American" or going to Europe and being loudmouth and insisting on water when people don't have it or all the crudenesses that we know *do* exist. That's not it; that's another situation altogether. This is simply a matter of how trustworthy can you be if come from this context. And I assure you, you can't be very trustworthy. Nobody trusts us. You *don't* have to talk about Vietnam. You don't have to talk about South America. You can talk about Nevada. That's much closer to home.

That's right here. The only reason why those Indians aren't guerillas is because *they are not westerners.* I mean western civilization types. They don't have any sense of that. They just don't want any part of it at all. They're not trying to overthrow national life. They have no sense of organization, *like* that. They're simply trying to be Indians.

Now those people who are trying to remain Indians in the, I suppose, the truest sense that now exists, are the culturalists or the traditionalists; the old men who still wear their hair in braids, who still insist on speaking Shoshoni; who will refer to other Indians with derision as *thinking like white men.* In other words, the progressives. The ones who would like to assimilate to some extent at least. Those people . . . exist in an utterly negative sense. They don't want anything to do with any national thinking. They don't think of this as a country. After all that's our word: America. You say, "Well you're American too. You're the first Americans." Nix. They're not the first Americans. They never were Americans. That's *your* word. You applied the word "American" to them. They don't know—that's some kind of Americanized Italian label. They're not even Indians, even more conspicuously. And they know that. They're not Indians. They're not Americans. They've got a word for what they are but you don't know that. Because you've never of course taken the trouble to find out what it is. And you couldn't pronounce it anyway. Shoshoni has a kind of "ah Kh Kh Kh Kh," an aspirate "ch" sound with everything. You can't really even hear it. So everything you bring to them is your notion of what they are. It's not theirs. And they, if you press them of course they'll tell you it's not theirs, the hipper ones. But mostly they won't even bother to tell you. They'll just look at you. They'll just look right at you.

[Pause. Back at blackboard.] Okay. Now, here, this is . . . Pocatello and Fort Hall Reservation is here. Fort Hall is one of the main points on the Oregon Trail. Oregon-California Trail came out here through South Pass and up here the Donner Party made the mistake, as you probably all know, of trying to go across the Wasatch and got lost . . . Fort Hall was where people went over and went down into the Humboldt or they continued on to Oregon. These people, the Northern Shoshonean speakers, are all called Basin-Plateau people. Paiutes are Shoshonean speakers. Bannocks, who are at Fort Hall, are Northern Paiutes. An important thing to understand is that these Indians are not those . . . fabulously acculturated, tricky cute types that you can run onto in the Southwest who . . . have made themselves attractive from . . . lots of points of view. I mean, there's a spectrum . . . I mean a wholly competent professional Indian to the real cultured Indian that you will find. But whatever that spectrum is, this is not the kind of Indian that the Shoshoni is, at all. He did not come under the sway of the Spanish. He was not taught silv— they never worked in silver. They made a few baskets, mostly deerskin. Mostly leather clothes and moccasins, beads. Beads were introduced by the trappers and Fort Hall was one of the main dissemination points for those. And so they learned a kind of bead craft. But they didn't throw any pots of any value. Again culturally . . . They didn't do *much* actually. They finally acquired the horse . . . and that allowed the Eastern Shoshoni to then go out onto the plain and make for himself a different economy with the buffalo . . . and he was fierce too. The Shoshoni was a dreaded horseman. For these other people down here, the horse never became really important. They got it, finally, as it came in, in the eighteenth century. But it . . . never moved them out onto the plains. This is the Eastern Shoshoni. The Western Shoshoni are at Duck Valley, which is right here. [Points to blackboard.] It's a fairly big reservation, about 500,000 acres. But that's all they got. Before that they were called Diggers. And that's a term of a program in American anthropology. It just meant, I mean, they dug camas roots and . . . other roots. And they gathered, too. They were gatherers also. And then they were jack rabbit hunters, small game. Because without a horse—and there weren't too many buffalo in there anyway, in the inter-montane region. So they're very much like people you would meet on the skidrow. They were like skidrow Indians. Not post-white but I mean pre-white. . . In other words they were poor Indians. Their economy was bad. Now Indians for the most part *were* rather limited to where they were. The Sioux successfully made the transition out onto the plains at a particularly opportune time for themselves. From the woodland to the plain, and everybody knows that. But . . . that's exceptional.

Even the Shoshoni religion, the most significant aspects had to come back from the plain. In the seventeenth century a group of Eastern Shoshoni split off and went to the Southwest, the Comanche. And they're Shoshonean speakers. And then about 1800 Omahamagwaya or Yellow Hand came *back* and brought the Sun Dance which had its big revival there in Wind River. And then spread across the mountains to—their relatives of those people at Wind River. It's a curing dance. So that became their most important thing. But never a rich culture in the sense that the eastern traveller who's after something to wear back home could come and respect what they were or what they did. Never that way.

And indeed, on the government maps for the reservation locations until just recently, about last . . . about last year I think, 1964, Fort Hall is the only reservation listed as "tourists not welcome." That means two things. They're not welcome because there's really nothing for them to do there except to look at Indians. And most tourists want to buy something actually. They don't want to just look at Indians. Especially if they're dirty poor Indians. And also the Fort Hall

Shoshoni didn't particularly want anything to do with white
people because the experience in Pocatello was very bad, had
been for a long time. Pocatello is not a very sympathetic
town to Indians. So the smarter ones, the traditionalists again,
the culturalists, stay on the reservation, rarely go to Pocatello.

Now at Duck Valley, here [points to blackboard], that's
Western Shoshoni. There are no, well there are a few Paiutes
there, I mean who can tell the difference. There is no difference really. They've all mixed by now. You'll find that that
place is richer. They have a lot of water. There's a place called
—there's a dam, the Wild Horse Dam in Nevada right here, in
the mountains. And the river flows all the way through the
valley. And it's a long and wide lush valley—lots of irrigation—
lots of Lombardy poplars planted by the first settlers in there
who were Mormons. And later kicked out, the place being
then restored to the Indians. So it has a beautiful aspect as
you look out over it. These tall slender trees placed around
on the farms. And they grow hay, almost exclusively. Some
of the best hay I understand in Nevada. And a lot of it. So
they're not so bad off. You find places where they have tele-
phones in their houses. And then of course they have tractors
and bailers and windrowers: everything to make hay with.
There are very few traditionalists at Duck Valley. There are
many more at Fort Hall. They've been forced back to the reservation, in a very real way. The Duck Valley people can go
off of it. They go to Boise and Elko. And they have money.
So in the sense that—not that they tried—but they have as-
similated. They have become part of America. Money will do
that. Whether you like it or not. Whether you want it or not.
I mean, the sheer power and force of money will make you
more American than you are without it. I certainly would say
that the most American Americans are—there must be some
ratio between how much money they have. For instance, the
man who is broke must be less American. He has to be. I

don't want to suggest that it's slightly un-American not to have money, but . . . I think the implication is there.

Well, alright, so the Indians come under that almost technical factor of how you are an American without even knowing it, or without even caring. After all, why should they care? They want—under these Lombardy poplars are the same shacks that you'll find in the ghettos at the edge of Elko and Lovelock, Winnemucca, Carlin, Carson City, Reno, Sparks. Same shacks. Same conditions—but they'll have a phone inside. Rarely a toilet. An Indian has to be really liberated in that part of the country to have a toilet because there is this notion that it's dirty and unseemly to go to the toilet in your house. *In* your house—you wouldn't, you don't do that. I mean the fact that it flushes doesn't really help, much. [Laughter.] The point is it went on there. And that's gotta be bad.

Well what I'm trying to say is that such an experience— say if, when it was proposed to me—I didn't have any particular interest in it. Any more than anything else. I'm interested in anything. Like I could walk out the door and go somewhere else. It doesn't really matter to me. I don't have any center in that sense. So if someone says, "Let's take pictures of Indians," I think, well, why not try it. And if it doesn't happen at least I'd like to talk to some Indians if possible. And if they don't talk that doesn't matter either. Just keep going and maybe you'll meet another one. But especially these Indians because they're not—they're off the road and . . . they— no matter how poorly they're doing it they do represent themselves at this stage. And this is rare. The Basin-Plateau is self-isolating.

Now on the way up to Duck Valley, Leroy and I stopped at a place called Mountain City. And there we met an Indian. Who, one could recognize immediately. His manner would allow one to read a great deal about him before he told you, or you asked. He had a cowboy hat on, one of those black things. All those hats are always turning up, like that. And he had levis and cowboy boots and had that western—he assumed that swagger. And he was drunk. Not drunk but I mean Indian drunk. The way they sort of walk like that. And the way they—their faces are almost masked with some kind of tension. And they're looking at you. And this funny English they speak. So he comes toward you. And he's playing the jukebox. And the jukeboxes are, you know, they're very hip. They got the Supremes and so forth—Rolling Stones, in those little towns. There's not, oddly enough—not country and western much. So he's doing that. He comes over, sits down and asks us if he can ride on to Duck Valley and we say "Sure." Be happy to have an Indian along. It's always safer to go with an Indian. But again, right off he's suspect. Because these people are divided in many ways. And that's another reason why they're very unlike—say their problems are very unlike—the problem of the American Negro. We knew right off that perhaps it's not like going in with just any Indian. But this is this particular Indian. For one thing he's a braggart, he's a firefighter, he's a rodeo performer who's really seen better days and now he's going to seed and it's dangerous for him—he gets busted up, his arm was messed up. And he's not going to be like the *best* recommendation to the authorities there, that we should be there to take pictures.

But anyway we took him and that night met his cousins. Who were all like him. Now they have a funny feeling of relationship to this country. For instance, they were let's see how old? Oh between thirty and thirty-five, I think. It's hard to say. They had been to the Korean *Conflict.* That was their big reference. And they referred to it as "conflict." They retained that propaganda device so effectively used at that time in the early fifties to avoid its being called a war. Right up to this time. That word. And you see, "Korean Conflict" is a very funny thing to hear coming from the lips of an Indian. I mean if somebody else said that to you you'd think, "Well wow." [Laughter.] But—an Indian. I mean you wouldn't per—you might not expect him to know better, that's not it. But you wouldn't expect him to say that. He might . . . he'd surely say something else. And they all said "Korean Conflict." Which again indicates how far out of the current news they are, too. Because the Korean Conflict, as the Vietnamese Conflict, is not being called a conflict anymore. Now it's a war. Everybody says, all the official organs refer to it as a war now. It's possible to change that last term after 1964, '63, because you can only have one conflict going at a time, obviously. There are many wars so then that, you know, got put in another bag. It's a war. Well they wouldn't have any sense of that. They didn't.

They drank white port by the half gallon. And a great deal. I've never seen such capacity, I don't think. They're all over the place. I mean we're driving all over the reservation wildly. It isn't like—you know any conception anybody might have of the wild life. Right there on the reservation. Really the wild life. And they were obviously the rowdy crowd, the do-nothings. When we would go by, it was late afternoon, we'd go by a field where a man, an Indian, was, you know, putting up his hay. They'd say, "Heyeyey, look at that." [Laughter.] Putting down his effort you know. Anybody working they put—oh wow, really—doesn't know what he's doing. "Come on come on," everybody was going. Small tight-knit group: hard core. Real rebels but inside nothing of course, *inside nothing.* Just inside their own Indian-ness. Never, never any relationship to what we might think of as a larger form of protest, involving some concept of the people as a whole. Never never that. But very good. Actually—I got very scared because they had guns and they were shooting them— [laughter] —you know—[laughter] —but I thought, "Take hold of yourself, Ed. You came here to see these Indians and now you've got to do it." The obligation became almost . . .

And then, well where we went was over to another ranch. Again cousins. By the way every time they move they have this phrase I noticed, "Down below, let's go down below." And they meant for everything, in every direction. Every radial you could possibly go in. Down below. "Well let's go down below and ride . . . you know ride this cow." Well they were very drunk. And needless to say we, both Roy and I pulled the cheapest of all whitemen's tricks and really faked the drinking. So, we weren't. We got there and they rode, they rode the cows. Which turned out to be Jersey milk cows. [Laughter.] But very *tough* Jersey milk cows. [Laughter.] And they could hardly get on. There was a beautiful girl, about eighteen, who smoked cigarettes constantly. But never took them out of her mouth . . . a lovely girl. And she—she wasn't drunk either, but she went along with the whole thing. Now there was a little, a very little girl—Mary was her name. About five or six who spoke very very good English. Very *nice* particular language coming out of her all the time. She told me that her mother would be very angry if she knew that these particular cowboy Indians were there drinking. So there was that going on too. The mother was away. These were real rowdies. Going around the univer—, the uh, university— [laughter] —the reservation—[laughter] —causing trouble. [Applause.]

Well it was kind of dark by that time and it was hard to get pictures. But these were the Indians who wanted their pictures taken. Once they relaxed and once we got to know each other they wanted their pictures taken. Not because they— you know it wasn't specious but they liked it. You know, they had an appetite for it. And we could satisfy it and get two things done at once. They felt funny about it. Because one man said to another, you know, "What are these guys taking pictures for?"... And this one Indian looked at him *very* seriously and closely and directly and said, "You want your picture taken. You wanted your picture taken." And that was very serious, I mean there was no—and so he was called. And he did want his picture taken. But he couldn't *quite* admit it. So there was this feeling that well, we're doing something dirty, on their part. And they were. They were doing something dirty by letting us take their pictures. We were doing something dirty by wanting to. They were going along with it and so were we. Every—that's one of the oldest American habits there is. Everybody's always doing something dirty and knowing it. I'm not pointing that out. I mean that was one of Lawrence's major themes, at least. But, one gets to think of it as some wildly literary fantasy of the mind that you know belongs in a book back somewhere. But it's right now and here. It's going on all the time. Always doing something dirty. And you call it understanding. Well, all right, let's understand these people better. You know, we'll get to know them through their images. And I believe that. It's true. I mean some of those pictures are going to be beautiful. But back of it there's a national strain that keeps it from being wholly beautiful. And it's in us. We can't and they can't.

Finally they fell off the cows. And the pictures were, you know—some of them didn't turn out. But then the photographer being black, and me, the writer being white fell out at that point. We had an argument. And that's predictable too. Because well Roy didn't want to look at it. You know, "For Christ's sake if these guys, you know they're going to kill themselves. If they want to do that let them go to Vietnam. You know—I don't want to see this. It's stupid." And he said, "What do you want to look at this for? What are . . ." And I said I want to look at it—it's not that but I mean this is ritual. And I see it right before my eyes and I want to look at it. This is the old—this is what—all they've got left, this is the vestige of that possibility of being a hero. OK, so it's riding a milk cow but they're taking a chance with their lives, which is very important to an Indian. And remains very important to an Indian. It's not important to us because we value our lives for some silly reason. We think death is some rather large event. We don't have the sense that death is simply an other occurrence, like any other occurrence that might happen on this *string* we call our lives. But they very much have that feeling. And they very much want to test this all the time. When is it going to happen? How tight is the string? What's on this particular segment of it? And death is not any, it's not any *great* thing. It's either there or it's not. And if it's not there then you know it wasn't, so you test it again. These people very much know that. So they do all sorts of dangerous things. Edmund Wilson in the back of that book—this anthropologist who talked about the Mohawk's particular ability to swing high steel in New York City, and the sharpness of their eyes. The ability to gauge distance without any surrounding reference. That is up three or four hundred feet in the air, or higher. Whereas we have to have the—like you know the glass is here so I can tell the corner's there. I don't think there's anything genetic about that. All of that idea that's pronounced in that book about how Indians do still want to test their own courage by very external means. That was what was happening to me. But on the other hand how can you argue again . . . I, as it turned out, it wasn't—I stayed and watched it but—and I don't yet know what I think of it. But I'll think something about it, later.

Okay. Those were those people. Now I kept trying to tell myself: I have to be here. I have to be there with the Indians. I don't have a country any more than they do. I'm like part of the Fourth World too. I, of necessity I have to be part of the Fourth World to retain any possible honor for myself. Which may be presumptuous, to want to honor *myself.*

They're part of the Fourth World. One speaks of the Third World, the underdeveloped nations. They're certainly not part of that. Any Peace Corps endeavor in their direction is right off ludicrous. They're at least a Fourth World. There may be other worlds. They're not even, well—we met a bourgeois Indian. He was something else. He worked at the . . . at Duck Valley there's a hospital, in there. The doctors who were not really Army I guess but they wore Army uniforms and had those same Major, Captain, Lieutenant insignia, worked for the Public Health Service at this hospital. They were all, well-fed and rosy and innocent and honest and decent—suspicious. [Laughter.] So their pictures were taken. And they told a little bit about the hospital, what they were trying to do and so forth. And the Indian who worked there . . . and had the use of a car I noticed, but he had no rank—was very affable and co-operative, interested: not suspicious like the ordinary reservation Indian because he figured us as good publicity for the tribe. For the, he—in other words you can smell that way of thinking. Like, well this is going to bring our problems before the nation. It's going to create an advertisement for us. So . . . that's good. So we went home to lunch with him. He had a white wife, a French woman that he had met in France and brought back to the reservation. She seemed completely indifferent to where she was or what was happening . . . and the children were beautiful. The house was neat, a model of efficiency, cleanliness. It had the look of a worker's house more than a middle-class house, much more. And I thought of some kind of scale in which—and his income by the way must have been pretty good. Because I suppose he made three or four hundred dollars a month from the government and has three hundred acres in hay. Which is a good income there, again. So he had a new pickup truck. It wasn't—the worker quality of the house was simply what happens, it seemed to me, when the Indian gets out of the absolutely dishevelled shack into something he conceives as approximate to a well-run American household. So that it didn't become middle-class. It didn't have that kind of pretension. It stopped lower on the scale from that. He had horses. He was very anxious to have his picture taken. And he—so he posed on his horse and so forth.

But then he told us of his great-grandfather who was still alive and a hundred and two years old. His wife was alive. He drew—and he thought that we very much should go over and visit with this man. A historian, a state historian had come down from Boise several years ago and done an article on the man. And it had been in the Boise paper. So he was sort of used to that sort of thing and was there as a figure of antiquity. So we said, "Sure, yeah." "We'll go over there. So after lunch we went over there using the map and got there through three gates or so. Which you have to open and close. They're barbed wire gates on posts with just wire to hold them. There were a collection of three shacks and it took us a while to find them. And I went around the back and to the screen door and the woman was there. And . . . I can't really express my shock at seeing her. She—I've never seen anyone older than a hundred years old. And she had a white, no blue, yeah it was a blue kerchief with white flowers around her head but down certainly across her eyelids like that. And so she looked up a little bit. And she didn't say anything except some Shoshoni [unintelligible guttural sounds] like that. And unlatched the screen and I went in. I mean I felt—I don't know. You know I mean I don't know whether she said get in or drop dead or—I don't know. I mean but she didn't pay any attention to me, just pointed into the next room where the man was. I went in and there he was. Certainly thinner than Gandhi at the end of one of his fasts or at least comparable to one of those pictures after the war in Poland or from one of those camps where people were—had their knees like that

and their legs that way. He was sitting on the edge of the bed.
Absolutely beautiful man with utterly sharp piercing eyes.
But the rest of him. Well the wrinkles you can imagine. You've
seen that approximately already. His hair was black *and* white.
No grey interspersed. Long hair. And he was dying. He said in
—he had a little bit of English, although it was disconnected
because he could hardly hear. And so he wasn't replying to
what you'd ask him or anything like that. But he described
that his troubles were in his chest here and around his back.
And his feet were really dirty: the whole place was very dirty.
Incredibly dirty. It was one of the dirtiest places I've ever seen.
I thought, Wow I—I don't—I don't know where I am. But
then I thought well, again, I'm here. So back to that. How do
you get around being where you are? Even though you went
to whatever you did to get there. You may question what
you did to get there but you're there, alright. So I tried to
talk to him and had to speak very close to his ear. Right up
almost my mouth touching his ear almost screaming. And he
could hear but then again he wouldn't reply to the question.
So it became obvious that we weren't talking. But still I, you
know, we tried. And every once in a while he would break
out in a *lovely* chant. In Shoshoni, which has a nice long line
to it. [Chants.] Like that—haaa—but deeper, you know. I
mean that's—I don't want that to be a parody or anything
like that. I thought it was a death thing you know, a death
chant. Because the wife would go over—she wanted to *die*
very badly—I mean she was *begging* to die. But she just, I
guess, couldn't. She went over, she would go over all the time
and lay on the edge of the bed and sort of curl up in a foetal
position. And right on—the only corner that she could possibly lay on because it was piled high with rags and a lot of
things. And then she would get up and go back: she was taking care of him. I mean she would then go over and speak in
Shoshoni to him, once in a while. They were, I suppose, try-

ing to get straight who we were, or what we were doing there. I mean 'cause there was no way to tell. I mean they must have been a little bit, oh I don't know, scared, maybe scared. Although they didn't have the energy to display it, any kind of fear.

The question in my mind all along was: now why had this man, the Public Health Service employee, the grandson, the great-grandson, why had he sent us over there? He had been there, he must have known what the place looked like. He must have known what—how these people were. I mean what . . . and again the calculations started going on. Like how we always try to calculate what reason do they have, you know, for doing something. We're always calculating that. And I was—my machines were running. And he's either —he can't be, he's not a stupid man. Because I talked to him. And at lunch he had told me what real respect he has for the traditionalists. That they use the language in the old sense with authority. That—say there's a man at Fort Hall, a famous traditionalist—Willie George is his name—is a great Shoshonean speaker and when he gets up to speak he speaks, in the old way. Which is to say that everything says something. The people of the last generation who have still been taught some Shoshoni in the household according to this man, very often *don't* say much with it. They can speak it but it's hit or miss. They may say something or they may not. It's kind of, yeah it's just hit—it's hit or miss. But these old men really—they speak all the time and they're saying something all the time. It has great weight and direction and authority and it's right there. Nothing—no slack at all. And he respected this. He was talking about it, in a very lovely way I thought. How he, although he was a progressive and wanted the, you know, the Indians to be better off. He liked this and would think it a shame if it died out, but that it *was* dying out. And so forth. So I mean—I had respect for him too and the way he felt . . .

I don't know, I thought perhaps, it might be the old man himself. Hundred two years old. And his wife. Maybe that after
all was their place. And no matter where else you might take
them that would *not* be their place. And they were dying.
They were performing the act of dying. And finally it didn't
matter *where* that happened. It was really beside the point.
I mean when I finally saw that—well I knew anyway. I'm not
scared by dirt in any sense. In fact I prefer it. I just can't
stand other people who like it.

   Alright. Let me get off that. What I'm trying to get to is
that no matter what—no matter how you find the Indian or
no matter who you are, no matter what your interest is, the
thing you come up against is the in—the inside of a nation: it
has a life, inside. And if you go out with someone—to someone, to meet someone else, *that's* a relationship. And then all
three of you, all three of those factors, have a relationship
with the whole thing. And it's always there. It's always there.
It's always there. You will find that everyone, every—everyone in the community is a cop, everyone is a policeman, every
woman driving a pickup truck is a policeman. Every one of
them. You can't ever make a mistake about it. They're all
part of the constabulary. They watch you. You're a stranger.
Why are you there? What right do you have to be in Nevada?
The sovereign state of Nevada. Or the sovereign local community of wherever it is. It can be the most podunk worthless
dryfaced town you could imagine. But they value that enough
to make the whole citizenry a constabulary. It must be obvious that in our national life, say taking it in the last fifteen
years, that this entire nation *is* one vast huge policeman.
There are only a few people to be policed. Just a few. In fact
there are so few people to be policed by this vast horde of po-
licemen that you know them all. You know who they are.
They are that few. They're recognizable. You know who
they are.

Well that leads to another thing then. On the reservation it's one thing say . . . if you're there. Because that's their land and their nation. They deal with the government by themselves. They're independent national entities, the reservation people. You go to small enclaves along Route 40: this is the Paiutes now. And you'll find that those people form a pool at the edge of town for *use* by the local citizenry whenever they want it. They're kept depressed. There's usually one street, a collection of hovels, and maybe fifty to two hundred, three hundred Indians. Now those people, if you try to go in and talk to them are going to be very very different. They don't even want to see you. They just think you're coming down to do something. Of course you are. You very much are. So *they* don't form part of anything at all. They're *not* an independent nation. They're *not* American citizens. They *don't* exist on this continent. They have no existence at all except in those hovels. And that's nothing. And believe me I'm not trying to argue any kind of sociological concern. At all. None whatsoever. They've had that too. It's simply the fact of existence. Relative to a small town that thinks well of itself, to which they can be of occasional help, on land that they once occupied, which was theirs, in the Basin-Plateau country, between the mountains. Now they are the most *wretched* of the earth. And without any possibility, forseeable at least, of coming together in some organized way. They're split by language and dialect. All through that one small area actually; because they're not all Shoshonean speakers in the intermountain west. They're split by what remains ritual differences. They're split by a hangover of wanting to fight each other too. Because what happens if you always went out—say if you used war as a dance, as a party, as entertainment, as a social form: war as a social form, with not too many people killed. Largely by accident. And that's missing then—but something else has come to replace it, namely drink. And in the case of Reno, dope. There are Indian junkies there. Which is a *pretty strange* thing to see. There are all sorts of other things that will be handed you to substitute for this once more coherent way of conducting your life and your relationship with your neighbors. War for them was a way of getting along, if it could be, if that can sound right. It kept things straight. And it allowed the young men to be some place. Now the young men can't be any place. It's a problem of the young men. I feel very much like an Indian in a way. Because I remember when I was a young man there was no place to be either. And again I mean to pick up what Bob [Creeley] said about—the war *is* a large reference for my generation, I'm sure. The end of it, not the war itself, because I was slightly too young to have gone to World War II. But that end of it where there was no place to be, the stream of G.I.'s coming back. The whole dishevelled nature of the United States at that point was—seemed to me very parallel to the problem of young Indian boys, off the reservation especially. On the reservation they can—there's some work to do. But otherwise no. They're really without any form. Even the most depraved of white Protestant American has a form. We almost understand that—even the most grotesque athletic youth of eighteen has a hotrod or knows somebody in the country club. Or does something, he has something. And it's part of the national fabric. He can do that. He can be there. It may be nothing that will give him any kind of strength. But it's something to occupy his life on earth until he waits for this moment he must dread.

Okay. Well those are some of the things I saw. Now I'd like—I want to ask myself if a poet exists except—except as he can *be* somewhere and *with* something. I really do think that . . . it's possible to have a poem. Yeah—a poem exists. We know that. But it's a much harder proposition as to whether a poet exists or not. Sometimes he does, sometimes he doesn't. He may or he may not. To my mind he has to *be there* as much as possible. In other words he has to discharge himself into the—some arena of life at least to the extent that—or trying to approximate the extent to which a poem can do that. And then he can be, I would say maybe nearly a poet. People can be nearly poets when they do this. Not people. Yeah, people. Anybody. People can, are poets when they *are* there with all of themselves. And that's—yeah that is a condition again to my mind, it's a possible condition. Never quite reachable, I mean *exactly*. But only, only *by* that condition can you have the force of a poem then. And a poem is force, that kind of force. Now I don't—the other part of it—I believe in the gods. In the sense that I—not that I have any particularly. I've thought a couple of times I did and they've come and gone. And they're certainly welcome. But other people do and you might be able to see them. I thought a couple of times with the Indians that I was close to gods I could respect. And heard them really. I mean certainly when the old man was chanting I thought—god *power,* very much. And several other times. And also . . . I don't really want to talk about that because I think everybody knows what that is.

Now, let me finish it off by talking about one more thing. I've got a note: the world and the uselessness of national boundaries. With the provision that any kind of one world idea is usually a trick of misunderstanding of what to be a whole world is. One world is not necessarily a whole world. It can remain the same conglomerate that we've got. I have no love at all for the state or any kind of nation but, on the other hand, I listen to anti-state arguments that strike me as stupid also. So I don't really know what to think of that. Except that it might be possible to have a world very shortly in which the *people* will start ignoring that apparatus that intervenes with us constantly and constantly hangs over our head

like that famous sword. To ignore it, in other words. I don't
think—as I think of it actively, I don't think that revolution
except in rather particular places, namely South America or
Southeast Asia, has any point. It has to be far more radical
and far more subversive than that. I think the people just
have to stop paying attention to that bullshit and turn their
backs on it. They have to start looking at each other. They're
doing that already. The state will become less and less important and it will—it won't even know it. I'm sure that the—say
the government of the United States doesn't really realize yet
that it's no longer a force in the world. And that it's no
longer important to the American people. It really isn't. It's
utterly beside the point. Now, the strength of its vast apparatus is another thing and that obviously continues to grip us
and will. But for . . . even practical purposes it is not necessary to have it any more and I—everyone *must* know that. It's
really just irrelevant. It's certainly irrelevant to anyone who
doesn't—who isn't American. And I would again maintain
that most of us are not Americans who think we have the possibility of living. Anytime someone comes through Pocatello
who looks like a criminal, or a fugitive, a bum, somebody
weird looking and it doesn't take much to be weird looking
in Pocatello, I immediately recognize them as the people that
I want to walk beside, to be near, to talk to, to be with. Because they are precisely the people who for one reason or another have compromised their allegiance to the thing that
might destroy us all, including them. And they've taken that
risk. Maybe they haven't taken it voluntarily. I don't—that I
don't care much about. But they maintain it. The man who
doesn't belong in a community is probably the man to pay
attention to. The old idea of the stranger is still very strong.
That's definitely a Greek idea. We may not honor him any
more. We don't. Because we don't have—we didn't inherit

that part of the culture unfortunately. But we certainly know who he is and the stranger's fearsome. He's the man to talk to. He's the man who knows where he's come from. Thank you. [Applause.]

[Pocatello-Berkeley, 1965]

Robert Creeley's *Pieces*

Pieces are a deliberate lyric of the emotional process. The deeply layered activity of qualitative information. If there is time, and the energy continuum of the reader's attention is not cut by the grammatical simplicities which largely move the poem around its corners, then the promise of the poem can be fulfilled. At least theoretically all the pieces can be found. This is an exotic technique. In Creeley's system the chair which sits in any kitchen waiting for the occupant who needs the combined warmth of the fire, the drink, the word is not a gratuitous social sentimentality (the long trail awinding, the light in the window), it is a precise social property. Back of the situation there are reams of documentation. Yet the poem is of a molecular constituency, never shorthand, and so each one is a model of a social universe located with a high degree of resolution. Held in place by an ear of such an order of strictness

> I have no ease
> calling things beautiful

> which are by that
> so called to my mind.

or by the fanatically balanced structures of cultural memory
one finds in the whole run of "Numbers," or, what is this?

> Here now *you* are—
> by what means?
> And who to know it?

a discrimination of sizable implication. Of course, there is no
"reason" to hear it as anything but the particular of an itali-
cized you. And yet one is cautioned by the *tone* to pay attention to the perspective of the meaning. If there is an earth
view in these poems, which with few exceptions are by no
means literal, it seems to be operated by a surfacing tone. Because it comes from some depth it isn't that "tone" which re-
veals so many seconds or arc on the occasion of a social event.
Not, in other words, how you might possibly speak. As if you
were the function of your own system. And could thus be
predetermined by some such scale.

> Here is all there is,
> but *there* seems so
> insistently across the way.

This verse is "big," in other words, by virtue of the distances
the rhetorical instruments can resolve and not at all in proportion to some incapacitating ratio of subject to object. The
linguistic force to be gathered by this means is difficult to
measure but one certain result is that the common mistake of
modern practice (i.e., the miscalculation of that ratio) is not
present. Anyhow, the poem as this book makes it in no case
depends on that measurement. There is a lingering phraseolo-
gy (not the same as memorable lines) which can suggest a
meaning for hours or years back of the leading voice. This
condition suggests there is an autonomy of person which par-

allels, as if the source were that remote, and is gathered with the poem, and sometimes, because it is difficult to keep track of two things at once, overrides its working, tampers with its escapement. And these poems are that finely made one might say *by hand* if that weren't, at this time, a qualified praise.

Yet parallel, or person, is perhaps not the point. The autonomy might be the effect of the poem

> Hearing it—*snivelling*—
> wanting the reassurance of
> another's decision.
>
> There is no one precedes—
> *look ahead*—and behind
> you have only where you were.

Any conceptualization should seek its own greatest simplicity, advice impossible to repeat too often:

> My plan is
> these little boxes
> make sequences. . .

Pieces have the implicit aim to find the whole of which they were and are now the signal. They should not be confused with fragments, which are self-contained entities, in the first place, of a special, and possible freak, nature. In this way marbles in an inscribed circle are pieces of the game, picked up until one has all the marbles of that occasion. Again, this is not precisely the same thing as saying you won. There are many ways to win. Some people win by losing, a widespread and sometimes vicarious habit. Fragments are nevertheless an invention of psychoanalysis to cover that case in which there never was a whole for that definition of a part. These pieces have no such unnatural affinities

> I want to help you

           by understanding what
           you want me to
           understand by saying so.

would disturb no one who wanted to be understood. Or, it
might. But that's why the strict quality of anything is art. It
isn't necessarily old-fashioned, this procedure, but there is no
questioning that it is traditional. It assumes an address multiple to itself. That is not exactly a modern assumption. Any
tradition comes forward in the form of the person carrying it.
Books lose track of it very quickly. It is not automatic that
poetry is art, even the greatest present poetry. It does not,
moreover, follow that personality is art, even the greatest present personality. *The* Art of poetry will choose to be born by
the agent of the greatest syntactical density in the language,
which we naturally call *the world.* It is true, and no contra-
diction, that the world has not been very precisely defined
since Shakespeare. The replification of the world is not interesting. It generates itself, if allowed. In *Pieces* the world
breath is a motion of real establishment. And the confronta-
tions, within the organism of their emotional time, are the
exactitude of the world insofar as it can be accurate.

           I want to help you
           by understanding what
           you want me to
           understand by saying so.

     Nobody writes like Creeley anymore than anybody
writes like Shakespeare. That is the art of perception. The
art of poetry is the same thing as the art of perception.

                                        [Chicago, 1970]

Of Robert Creeley

One of the most notable characteristic behaviors of late american verse is that it spins away from its center. There is a cen-
trifugal "force" inherent in its necessity to compose itself
while it simultaneously disregards the decomposition of its
own structure. The frantic recycling of the strategies against
hopelessness drags language in its wake. The shiny illusion
that there could be such a thing as american language, apart
from peculiar utterance, was never very promising. Thus, one
of the main functions of verse practice here has been to de-
monstrate speech. Oratory served this function for a long
while from another position.

For all the effort to check this drift through the agency
of specific reference, largely imported from the vocabularies
of lump science, there is little to indicate that the errant
breeding of surface language is either qualified or tamed and
what integration has been effected has been done at the ex-
pense of control. Quite an unhappy state, and reiterated by a
boredom throughout communications. In this condition, the

wisecrack is about as great as the voltage gets. That's why, of course, the news always ends with a casual joke.

Creeley's advancement on Williams has been radical: he discharged the soft locus of that attention and proceeded directly to the bone of human transaction. Creeley has not been exercised by local geopolitical observation and this freedom has purified his art to a fineness which is unique in the vastly abulic expression of our time, wherein the authority of the tongue has been expropriated by the mouth. He is the master of immediate speech and this is the compass of his written art, the speech provides all that is parabolic and exploratory, a speech of swift scansion, where the suggestion of totality is held with a light, confident grip, which we then have rendered in the poems.

[Boulder-San Francisco, 1978]

Night 65,
300 Nights to Come

The Garrick Ohlsson program of March 5th 1971 began at
7:45 with a trip on the el. A moist warm evening. We sat on
the platform over the Parkway and made some smoke. Jenni-
fer whispered isn't it strange how much this looks like a tur-
kish cigarette? I think we should smoke it like a cigarette.
The train arrived and opened its doors. As the car jogged
along we were held on a vision which lay between the shining
rails and which prostrated itself before a nearby infinity to be
called Chopin. Like chunks stuck together. I mean it was really grotesque.

    We reached the Auditorium Theatre at 8:15 and quickly
moved into the lobby. Sat down on a stone bench by the
stairs, had some tobacco and a paper cup of orange juice.
Then up to section FF. The Steinway stood brute silent on
the stage, mouth propped open with a wooden stake. The
boy comes in with an old-fashioned beard on.

    The first number is Soneto 104 del Petrarca with one
bow and then Sonata in F minor, Opus 5 with some prema-

ture coughing and applause between the Andante and the Scherzo and some mistaken applause between the Scherzo and the Intermezzo, followed by two bows. Mr. Ohlsson's exercise not surprisingly laid the foundation of the following comparative: Liszt has a head heavier than Brahms.

During the intermission we line up with 35 ladies from Miami who are shouting "The music is Everything" and ten minutes later we arrive at a niche in the wall which turns out to be the house of a skinny arc of water.

The first number this time is the Triptych of Louis Weingarden. The composer was drunk when his allegory seized him. The virtuoso does what he can, but it is a house-piece. A few rows down a group of college music teachers pass a folded sheet of paper between them which evidently has a joke written on it. A 12 year old boy sitting across the aisle is asked to leave by the listeners in his territory and he climbs the stairs with his head in his hands outstretched before him.

And now it is time for Chopin! Nocturne in E-flat Major, Opus 55, No. 2 is dressed pretty but soon humdrum. Scherzo in E Major, Opus 54's a bitch. Polonaise in F-sharp Minor, Opus 44 begins with the zest of a Russian and ends with the solidity of a Pole. Just the right truck to bring around for the move home. And we chant moving through the lobby and the encore, Goodbye Garrick, Goodbye.

[Chicago, 1971]

Semi Gross: Thoughts on the U.S. Open, 1978

When the Australians altered tennis some years back by concentrating on power, they "changed the game" so that finesse took a long nose dive and struggle replaced art.

Winning or losing Borg looks better than Connors because Borg's game is visually interesting. When Connors says he loves us even if we don't love him he's thinking of a lusterless style, and doesn't really care whether Jimmy is likable or not.

The quality of the talk has fallen right into line with the general cheapening of the game, and the "net" result is a mere pre-zentation. Voice of Tony Trabert: John McEnroe's tempo just in his walk has slowed down, seems to me to be dejected. Next voice: Connors' tempo has picked up! Boy! what a turnaround. I gotta think he's gonna cross the next one. There's a lotta Tension. The crowd is getting some of the tension. I'd like to see a good bread & butter service right here. That's what McEnroe is thinking, where am I gonna serve this one this time. To me it's amazing how in sports it can change so quickly. He needs more punch, he shoulda punched that one. There's a lotta roadwork action around the baseline.

Since there is no reason to do otherwise, one assumes the word Punch is being used as in Bagwork. This running judgment has all the aural appeal of a wet jock strap hitting the lockeroom floor. A tennis crowd is inherently watchful. It is a game to follow, the connection between the player and the crowd is concentration. Concentration is important in other games from the crowd's standpoint but it is dis-continuous, as in baseball, as in football, as in most team sports, except occasionally soccer, and sometimes hockey.

But if this palaver is more woodheaded than an astronaut's sub-verbal survey of the moon, when the women come on we get rushed back inside the cave.

But in the meantime there are even more things going on. In fact, this entire "event" seems to be in the hands of an even greater soundtrack coming from somewhere above. The outrageous Jet-trash filters not-so-gently down from the heavens in excruciating almost regular waves. When this unavoidable backsky (one can't truthfully call it back*ground*) was alluded to, the promoters "of this excellent facility" actually took the Large View that since jetnoise overload is a fact of life in the seventies, the condition here in Flushing Meadows is actually *better* for capturing one of the biggest typical mass disturbances of our time. Even slight reflections on this "amazing" point of view could make one regret the provision of a soundproof booth for the announcers.

Because what came out when the women came on was *Truly* amazing. The attitude of B.J. King raises serious questions about the plea for equality if her mouth is a sample of the idea of fairness. And precisely as it is conveyed on a national instrument. The really distasteful attacks launched against Pam Shriver by King ("separates the girls from the women," after a lengthy exchange Shriver lost) were nicely supplemented by Evert's resolute non-acknowledgment of the jet interference. She was consistently referred to as "cool." But when it came time to receive the trophies, the voices (insofar as one could hear them) were categorically clear: the voice of Evert that of a girl (behind Peyton Place cosmetics) and the voice of Pam Shriver that of a young woman.

The really big irritation however, to put those discriminations aside, was that a moment of brilliant youth, something no nation can live without, was diminished by a senior player with all the wit of a tennis shoe.

[Boulder, 1978]

Fear and Clothing
at the Blue Note

Notes on a fashion show

Make passes at you, do they?
Why, then, don't you wear clothes
that don't so accurately outline
what they're interested in?
—Guy Davenport's *Diogenes,* frag. 107

Saturday night is the next to the loneliest night of the week.
A drifting performer mountebanks a small crowd from the
entryway of a shoe store. Further west, outside the entrance
of the Blue Note, where the grass looks like a thousand dogs
just passed through on their way to Nederland, a far larger
lumpenboulder crowd is staring mooneyed at anything that
moves. The most anonymous shuffler is given a scrutiny that
would meet the standards of M.I.T.

What a suggestive entrance to a fashion show!

The door to the Blue Note was open on that August evening: a bad sign for air conditioning. Having walked by a mob
of ticket takers whose indifference to our outstretched tickets

was as total as an eclipse, we mounted the ramp to the interior. You could have served the air with a ladle. The mercury was threatening the top of the tube. A Blue Note crowd is a wondrous thing. Whereas other establishments more or less maintain a predictable clientele according to their peculiar lights, in the Blue Note the rocks and the discs all roll together. And there is even a kind of polyestero-denim mutation in evidence.

The atmosphere is lively enough, and while settling ourselves we let our minds wonder what would be the most appropriate, strongest nonknockout drink with which to spend the evening. To our considerable dismay we discover that the fifteen-dollar ticket price does not include drinks.

Before the fashion show starts there is time to scan the overall set. The tacky ramp, hastily covered with red wrinkle, brings Tijuana to mind. The wandering photographer reinforces this impression. The M.C. starts the evening: "The first walk we're going to take tonight is into a little bit of *black* and *white.* Good evening Ladies and Gents, Welcome to Night Moves!" Boulder cool.

Sitting in the center with good seats overlooking the floor turned out to be less an advantage than we thought. Since the ramp was narrow and came out from the stage twenty feet at the most, the models lined up behind each other, single file, allowing most of the room only a "domino view" of the action.

If the sponsors couldn't manage wings to scatter the promenading groups, they could have devised a functional choreography. Charlotte's Silks from Nicoles could have slipped to the floor like swans, each revealing the next number in the corps de couture.

The solos and pas-de-deux were on the whole more of a pleasure to watch. For a start they could be seen.

Susie in the Feather Dress was good. Billie's cool, modulated, and highstreet walk made anything she wore look great. Beata, a cold Breck Girl, had the most class. As cold as the Yukon, delicada, with strong bone structure. Kelly made the show feel like a party. Dancing along with the music of Flying Wedge, she had the force to dominate polka dots and to make the new designer airforce uniform by Bonnie less than military.

The guys were all equally terrific. Pierce and Jason looked real loose in Oxford shirts and red silk ties by Curtford.

Maggie was tough in Charlotte Ford's Champagne dress. A sleek "she's got Datsun in her eyes" look.

As for the Styles this year, or the favorites chosen by Last Tango, Livoni, and Scarpaletto (women, men, and shoes) they are classy (silk) but casual (not high fashion).

Loose, slightly pegged pants are in. So are French pockets (French meaning deep side splits on either hip).

The furry detail of a costume hung with tails haunts my mind like adventure (i.e., a raid on radio antennae in an Arkansas parking lot?).

The skirts and dresses, like the pants, fall from a slightly gathered waist to a narrower (although variable) hemline. Just cut a slit in your skirt and you've got it. Legs are emphasized and subtly displayed in a swinging walk. Breasts are not quite out, but the square neckline with thin straps leaves little possibility for the plunge.

The style displayed here, with its variations, could be put at *slick low,* more or less expensive rack. Most of it is a smart and attractive shift in the sexual insinuations. The trouble with the mini skirt, remember, was that good knees are always in short supply, not to mention the trouble with a head-on view of a 25 lb. thigh. The slit controls these problems and in the case of the knee pretty much gets rid of them. A glimpse of the whole leg is apt to be much more attractive since it relents, and in the meantime, the long, flattering side view obviates some of the vagaries of evolution.

Fashion is high or low, let's face it. Middle, no matter what the prevailing habit, is never fashion. In fact, because it derives from puritan rather than aristocratic power, middle is anti-fashion. The middle realms are the uniformed civilians, from Lord & Taylor to Pendleton. They don't so much dress as get into an anxious fit. And of course there are always styles that fall entirely outside the domain of public promotion. For instance, in the matter of sheer personal expression, nothing rivals the dress of Geronimo's Band in eighteen eighty-six.

The punk shot, the show's finale, was disappointing—a hint that a punk doesn't buy his fear or his clothes at The Last Tango or Livoni's. A parody of what nobody wears, it was a dress-up time and anathema to style, whereas "punk" does actually have a style that romanticizes the 50s rebel and is only outrageous as far as it's sharp.

At the Blue Note, the concept of "punk" as conveyed by Boulder merchants looked more like "camp"—although to be fair, by that time, our eyeballs were slipping below table level. The Blue Note has a very blunt floor.

[Boulder, October, 1979]

Dog Eat Dog

Scene: 7-11 parking lot. A woman
in a Ford pickup slides to a halt,
the dust, not having any brakes,
passes over the rig. The window
cranks down. The woman whips the
barrel of a 45 out the window.
The head of a slinking orphan dog
explodes into the wind, its body
lifts 5 feet off the ground. Up
goes the window as a ball of dust
rises from the spinning rear wheels.
This phenomenon is called Target
Practice.

It may be true in a place longing for something to occur that
a dog fight will draw a crowd, but in Wyoming where the only
thing that's supposed to occur is a mineral strike, the dogs
better stay out of the way. In any case they haven't got time
to fight much. The leftovers from what the population eats
would put the dogs at risk, so a lot of them take to the road.

Wyoming is in its way a boom for dogs. And dogs are booming. They're hanging out close to the coyotes. If there are any dogs reading this, they should know that fresh killed meat is plentiful all along the verges of this simple, monumental highway system. Not just the plethora of antelope, deer, jackrabbits, beef, and sad to say, other dogs, but come summer, fresh snake.

And this further observation can be conveyed to the dogs. Wyoming is not a village world. Unlike in Mexico where the pack is tolerated, Wyoming is a collection of knots on an endless line. Along that line whip the Diesel Hordes hitting anything that gets in the way. They are the moguls of machines. Buffalo are dense enough to send a big rig over the edge and are therefore carefully fenced. All a dog has to do is stay on the line for an around-the-cloth banquet of protein by the ton and of a quality that would make Dr. Ross turn green. Not since the freezer compartment was accidentally left open for the weekend have the dogs had it so good. And this bill of fare will increase on a graph rising with extraction. The more you turn up the waves, the better it will be for Wyoming's Boom Dogs.

Is it any wonder then, that dogs are the most assassinated of our brother mammals in a state which loves target practice just a *leetle* better than its best friend?

[Boulder, 1979]

134

The Tower

Out in the terra nullius northeast of Gillette, Wyoming, is some of the most bracing category-A landscape left in the world. Contoured by strong suggestion rather than a conflict of masses, it is a piedmont loosely clothed with juniper and pine, with cottonwood and an abundance of shrub in the draws. The air is superb. A few people live up here, as well they might because it looks like a very good place to be. There is a steep drop-off in vehicular absurdity, habitations look competent and well-off but refreshingly ordinary. And in this domain of cattle there is very little road-kill.

Once in the hills and rising through the timber one instinctively expects a sighting around every open curve. It is a surprising long time coming but then, there it is, about a foot of the top showing the cracked mud capitals of the columnar fluting. And then it is gone from sight for another long while. The next view frames the whole majestic pillar of lava. And it is both modest and distant. In the same moment it is grandiose. This silo is in a class by itself.

Devil's Tower to us, Mateo Teepee, or Great Bear Lodge, to others. But the Dakota word *tipi* is more a tent dwelling than lodge. This tower is still here because Theodore Roosevelt, the man Alaska can blame everything on, declared it the first National Monument. It even has its own taped guide going into your car radio. The 75 feet of top we saw down the road is patterned by the shrinking which occurred when the lava cooled, about sixty million years in the past.

The atmosphere on this day late in March is as sparkling as a pocketful of stardust. It is midmorning when we arrive in the parking lot at the base of this tremendous menhir. Across the way a group of climbers are sorting out their gear, making chimes of the metallic paraphernalia.

The trail around the base is a mile long. Designed to be an easy stroll, at this season a good part of it is under snow in the tremendous north shadow. On the south side of the base there is a slight, projecting park of smallish ponderosa. This was a flaking sight, perfectly accommodating a tedious occupation with a vast overview. From the tower there is an everlasting flutter of doves sprinkled with the hammering of pitons.

Words like cathedral, much less stump, do not describe this singularity. If it resembles anything back on Earth it would be the Acropolis, and then only in the high-quality rubble about its base. These immense piles are the fallen columns, three to eight sided, but usually six. It makes one feel like a bug crawling over them. At this moment of sun we entered the shadow and felt the chill of eclipse in the northwest quarter. There is a direct sense of a cast of great size.

On a homelier level, there *is* this tendency to gawk at it like it was a New York skyscraper. The neck breaks from its urging of the eyes to look up, again and again. The literature says there is a small community living at the top, which is about an acre and a half in extent. Grass and shrubs fed upon by chipmunks, pack rats, and mice. The eyries of prairie falcons are the stabilizers. Saturday night must be wild on the summit.

Circle complete, a strong sun warms us up in the parking lot. The drive down is thoughtful, through a series of easy drifts. Cognition has been washed and lightened. There seems no question of the remote and special tranquility of this awesome formation. There is still a tangible vibration lingering from its terrible birth.

[Boulder, 1979]

H₂O:
A Review of Many Waters

Of all the common luxuries, water drinking has been the most
diminished by the foul habits of man for the longest time, far
far longer than the corruption of the air. Hunting and skinning
disqualifies the water enormously even within the perimeters
of such low-scale activity as that now seems. Irrigation is a
major disturbance. And everybody is an expert on industry.
Water, in fact, degrades itself depending on where it's been,
and such is the nature of water that it can go practically
everywhere.

Strictly speaking, water is the oxide of hydrogen, and has
no more character than paraffin, which it was once thought
to resemble structurally. When water is sweet and light and
clear of interference it smacks of the best parts of the earth.

A short while ago Prince Faisal announced his intention
for the tenth time to tow icebergs from the Antartic to Ara-
bia. He said "the iceberg" (and presumably he has one in
mind) would amount to a flow twenty-two times the Nile. He
didn't say for how long. At any rate, much of South Polar ice

is shoddy in composition and inferior in quality, being mixed with sea-ice and compacted neve. Some of the southern bergs extend half their bulk above the surface. They would probably not sink the *Titanic*. The heavy, high gloss bergs are bobbing in the North, out of the Prince's reach. A quicker-witted Europe would build an aquapipe to trade the Prince water for light crude, gallon for gallon.

Really pure water is blue when viewed through a considerable thickness. All waters, unless very impure, are made safe by boiling, but some waters are so rich in bacteria that a pressure filter which is supposed to burst the organism, plus boiling, is no guarantee against the ravage of water. There is a bug in Mexico which has three heads and can get past all present barriers into the gut where it hangs on with one head and eats with the other two.

That's bad, but the cure is possibly worse. No thinking human should drink Boulder water without boiling it. Chlorination presents some strange problems entirely aside from the aesthetic consideration arising from greenish yellow gas with an irritating smell and destructive effect on the respiratory tract. Yet Boulder city tap water is probably safe to cook with because chlorine, the recently discovered vector for radiation, is volatile, although no one can vouch for the safety of bystanders. Perhaps the ancient observation "a watched pot never boils" should be the excuse for staying away.

There are several things wrong with Perrier water, aside from the fact that any goof can use it to wash his Sportster. It is bottled under pressure, in itself an unspeakable thing to do to water. The gas is removed to accommodate some kinks in the technique and then returned as the cap goes on, and it is claimed this gaseous sleight of hand makes no difference. That's for anyone to judge. Polish waters are nice. The Romans prized Yugoslavian waters and you can still get those from the same places.

The local water I like the most is Deep Rock. It is very light and very old, from ancient aquifer accumulations, and it's still oddly cheaper than gasoline. But there is no doubt which would fetch the higher price from a traverser of the desert. Deep Rock has a geological sharpness and clarity to it which allows you to abandon medicine. In these parts, the wisest check you can write is to Dan the Water Man.

The very highest water I ever personally tasted was taken from the stream about two hundred feet below the face of Eklutna Glacier, 75 miles northeast of Anchorage. Diamond blue, all the way to the Pleistocene.

SHORT SIPS FROM THE ANCIENTS

"Sir Isaac Newton defines *water,* when pure, to be a very fluid salt, volatile, and void of all savour or taste; and it seems to consist of small, smooth, hard, porous, spherical particles, of equal diameters, and of equal specific gravities; and also that there are between them spaces so large, and ranged in such manner, as to be pervious on all sides. Their smoothness accounts for their sliding easily over one another's surfaces; their sphericity also keeps them from touching one another in more points than one; and by both these their friction in sliding over one another is rendered the least possible. Their hardness accounts for the incompressibility of water, when it is free from the inter-mixture of air. The porosity of water is so very great, that there is at least forty times as much space as matter in it; for water is nineteen times specifically lighter than gold, and consequently rarer in the same proportion."

Johnson's Dictionary, the sixth edition

"For water is a moving, wandering thing, and must of necessity continue common by the law of nature."

Blackstone

"Theophrastus, in his work *On Waters,* says that Nile water is very fertilizing and fresh. Hence it loosens the drinker's bowels, since it contains a soda ingredient. He further says that many bitter waters as well as salt water and entire rivers change their character; such is the river in Caria on the banks of which stands a shrine to Zenoposeidon. The reason is that many thunderbolts fall in that region. Other waters, again, are like solids, and have a considerable density, like the water of Troezen, for it is no sooner tasted than it becomes a mouthful. The waters near the mines of Mt. Pangaenum weigh in the winter time ninety-six drachms to the half pint, while in summer they weigh forty-six. Cold weather contracts it and gives it a greater density. Hence, also, water flowing in water clocks does not correctly give the hours in winter, but makes them too long, since the flow is slower on account of its density.

". . . snow water is thought to be good, because the more potable element is drawn to the surface and thus broken up by the air; it is, therefore, even better than rain water, and water obtained for ice, also, is better because it is lighter; the proof is that ice itself is lighter than water in general. But cold waters are hard because they are more solid, and whatever is corporeal is warmer when heated and colder when cooled. For the same reason water on the mountains is better to drink than water in the plains, because it is mixed less with solid matter. For example, the water in the lake at Babylon is red for several days, while that of the Borysthenes at certain periods is violet-coloured, although it is extremely light. The proof: when the north wind blows the river rises higher than the Hypanis because of its lightness.

"When I had weighed the water from the Corinthian spring Peirene, as it is called, I found it to be lighter than any other in Greece. For I have no faith in the comic poet Antiphanes, when he says that Attica, besides excelling other places in many respects, has also the best water. His words

are: A. What products, Hipponicus, our country bears, excelling all in the whole world! Honey, wheatbread, figs. — B. Figs,
to be sure, it bears in plenty. A. Sheep, wool, myrtle-berries,
thyme, wheat, and water. Such water! You'd know in a minute you were drinking the water of Attica."

From *The Deipnosophists* by Athenaeus

[Boulder, 1979]

Four Seasons Books

ROBERT CREELEY
The Charm: Early & Uncollected Poems
Contexts of Poetry: Interviews 1961–1971
A Quick Graph: Collected Notes & Essays
Was That a Real Poem & Other Essays

EDWARD DORN
The Collected Poems, 1956–1974
Interviews
Views

DRUMMOND HADLEY
The Webbing

DALE HERD
Early Morning Wind and Other Stories

PHILIP LAMANTIA
The Blood of the Air
Touch of the Marvelous

MICHAEL McCLURE
Ghost Tantras

PAMELA MILLWARD
Mother, a Novel of the Revolution

CHARLES OLSON
Additional Prose
The Fiery Hunt & Other Plays
Muthologos: Collected Interviews and Lectures

DAVID SCHAFF
The Moon by Day

GARY SNYDER
Six Sections from Mountains and Rivers
    Without End, Plus One

CHARLES UPTON
Time Raid

PHILIP WHALEN
The Kindness of Strangers
Off the Wall: Interviews
Severance Pay

EDWARD CONZE (tr.)
The Perfection of Wisdom in Eight Thousand Lines
    & Its Verse Summary